THE NIGHT
OF THE COMET

OTHER YEARLING BOOKS YOU WILL ENJOY:

THE NIGHT
OF THE COMET

A Comedy of Courtship
Featuring Bostock and Harris

LEON GARFIELD

A Yearling Book

Published by
Dell Publishing
a division of
The Bantam Doubleday Dell Publishing Group, Inc.
666 Fifth Avenue
New York, New York 10103

The trademark Yearling® is registered in the U.S. Patent
and Trademark Office.

ISBN: 0-440-40070-8

Reprinted by arrangement with Delacorte Press

Printed in the United States of America

September 1988

10 9 8 7 6 5 4 3 2 1

CW

FOR PATRICK HARDY

Chapter One

LOVE turns men into angels and women into devils. Take Cassidy, of Cassidy & O'Rourke, Slaters, Thatchers, General Roofers and Sundries. He was a liar, a rogue, and so light-fingered it was a wonder that, while he slept, his hands didn't rise to the ceiling of their own accord. Whenever there was a night without a moon, suspicion naturally fell on Cassidy.

Yet there he sat, in the back of the cart, as good as gold and singing of Molly Malone and her wheelbarrow, and cockles and mussels, alive, alive-o! While O'Rourke did all the work.

It was early on the Wednesday after Easter and four days before the comet. The sun was as bright as knives.

"There's somethin' in the air, O'Rourke!" said Cassidy suddenly, with a sniff like a gale going backwards.

"Fish," said O'Rourke. "Stinking fish."

Cassidy shook his head. He sniffed again and went

as pale as it was possible for one of his complexion, which had something of brick, something of slate, and a good deal of the weather about it.

"'Tis the place!" he whispered. "I feel it in me bones, O'Rourke. What's the name on the signpost? For pity's sake, tell me, O'Rourke!"

It wasn't that Cassidy was hard of seeing. Far from it. In the old days he could have picked out a silver sixpence in a farmer's fist fifty yards off. It was just that he traveled propped among bundles and sacks with his face pointing backwards, so it would have been a great effort for him to sit up and turn around.

"Brighton," read out O'Rourke, a long, bony, melancholy man, with hands and feet the size of spades.

"Brighton!" repeated Cassidy with a sigh, as if that one word encompassed all the hopes of journey's end.

A year and a day they'd been going, in their old green cart with a pony that looked as if it had come through a storm of dapples and never been wiped down.

They'd jerked and jingled down every street of every town and village from Liverpool all the way around to here and now. They'd stared up into every window and knocked on every door, looking and looking for a girl by the name of Mary Flatley, who'd made an honest man of Cassidy by the contrary means of stealing away with his heart.

She'd gone from Dublin one fine day (that was the blackest in Cassidy's life), with bag and baggage and left not a word behind, except, "Tell that smarmy villain Cassidy I'm gone to England to make me fortune and get a husband who'll not gawp and drool at everythin' in skirts! Tell him I'm done with him—the dirty philanderin' rogue!"

She must have loved him dearly to have had such a devil of a temper where he was concerned.

"In Dublin's fair city, where girls are so pretty," sang Cassidy, regardless of the fact that such a state of affairs had been his downfall.

"I first set me eyes on sweet Molly Malone!"

While O'Rourke, who was strong on Sundries, boomed, "Tiles and slates! Chairs to mend! Pots, kettles, and pans!"

The cart turned down a little street of flint-cobbled houses that sparkled like trinket boxes in the sun. Cassidy gazed up at the windows, but O'Rourke stared down at the ground.

Such was his nature. He was a gloomy man, whose very name sounded like a raven's croak: *O'Rourke! O'Rourke!*

Every night, while Cassidy slept, he went around the graveyards with a lantern, reading the tombstones in the hope of not finding Mary Flatley under one of them.

Many was the sexton and late-night walker who'd seen the bony figure glimmering among the inscriptions and mournfully shaking his head.

"Are you looking for somebody in particular?"

"That I am. And may the flowers I'll lay on her grave not show their ugly faces above the ground till after me dying day!"

It would have killed Cassidy if he'd known what O'Rourke was up to, but somebody had to do it. For how could Mary Flatley turn out to be alive if nobody had made sure she wasn't dead?

They stopped at the first house. Cassidy smartened himself up and went around to the side, while the two brass buttons on the back of his old green coat kept a sharp watch on O'Rourke in case he decamped.

Not that O'Rourke would really have left him, even though he'd sworn that, one of these fine days, Cassidy would come back and there in the street waiting for him would be no cart and no O'Rourke.

Cassidy knocked, and a maid, armed with a coal shovel, opened the door.

"No hawkers!" said she, pointing to a notice Cassidy might have seen for himself if he'd had eyes in his head.

"And quite right, too! But on me honor, I've never dealt in hawks in me life, the terrible, sharp-eyed things! Have ye a hole in yer roof or a chair that needs mendin', me darlin' with the cherry lips and black-berry eyes?"

Cassidy had kissed the Blarney stone, all right, but by the squashed-in look of his nose, it must have been more of a collision than a kiss. There was none of your cheap good looks about Cassidy.

"Be off with you, you no-good Irish loafer!" said the maid, brandishing the coal shovel and preparing to shut the door, preferably with some portion of Cassidy in it. How was she to know that Cassidy was an angel now?

"Are ye acquainted," asked Cassidy hopefully, "with a lass by the name o' Mary Flatley? She's black hair and green eyes and a look on her that would bring

Dublin Castle tumblin' down. Mary Flatley—though she might be wed to another, and I pray to God that she ain't, for she's been gone a year and a day, so she'll be just after eighteen!"

But the door had slammed long before he'd finished, so it was to the hardhearted wood he called out, "If ye should happen to see her, just say that Cassidy's come!"

He went back to the cart, and O'Rourke, who undertook all expressions of a gloomy nature, sighed. Nobody could have expected Cassidy to have done it for himself.

They applied at the next house, but with no more success, and so on all the way down the street. At last they came to a well-appointed residence with a pair of anchors propped up on either side of the front door; which seemed to declare that the owner would go no more a-sailing and had dropped those articles for good and all in a neat green harbor with a gravel path leading up to the front door.

Cassidy cleaned his nails on his teeth and went around to the side. He knocked, and a female, all sails set, came to the door on a gust of freshly ironed linen. Cassidy took a step back. He felt she could have blown him clean out of the water.

"D'ye need yer roof mendin', ma'am?"

"I'll ask the master."

She shut the door and went away. Cassidy tried the door, but it was only from force of habit. The female came back.

"The master says there's two tiles off at the back. He'll give you five shillings to make it all shipshape and Bristol-fashion. But no thieving, mind! The master's a magistrate, so watch out!"

"Me thieve from you, ma'am?" said Cassidy, who could no more keep from courtesy than a cat from cream. "Why, 'tis me own heart ye'll be thievin' from me! But tell me, are ye acquainted with—"

The door was shut before he could so much as say "Mary."

He went back to the cart and told O'Rourke.

"A magistrate's house? No good will come of it, Cassidy."

"But it's the one, Mr. O'Rourke! It's the house!"

"How d'ye know that?"

"I feel it in me bones!"

"I'm warnin' ye, Cassidy."

"And I'm tellin' ye, O'Rourke. She's here!"

They took a pair of ladders off the cart and carried them around to the back, where a moldy old ginger cat fled at their approach and took refuge in an apple tree.

O'Rourke lashed the ladders together, and, when raised, they reached about two feet below the eaves. Cassidy began to mount. O'Rourke had no head for heights and consequently was always full of admiration for Cassidy's daring.

At every window Cassidy paused for a glimpse of the girl who'd have brought Dublin Castle tumbling down, while, below, O'Rourke prayed she'd not turn out to be high up, as the sudden sight of her would surely have done the same for Cassidy.

As Cassidy climbed, he leaned from side to side to take in a window almost out of reach. Sometimes he clung to the ladder with only one hand, so that, in his long green coat, he looked like a tottery caterpillar waving at the edge of a leaf.

From time to time he'd nod and raise a courteous finger to his head in recognition of having been caught looking in by somebody looking out.

In a lower parlor he saw the master of the house, a fine-looking old gentleman with seafaring eyes. Himself was sitting in a high-backed chair, and his poor gouty foot, all in a winding-sheet of bandaging and looking like the Raising of Lazarus, was sitting in another.

Cassidy saluted him, and the old gentleman scowled and made several upward jerking movements with his stick. Cassidy continued and at intervals saw and was seen by the tremendous female who'd answered the door and who seemed to be floating upward inside the house, like a wandering balloon.

He saw the lady of the house, a fine figure of a woman, who came to her window and asked him what the devil he was doing. Cassidy said he'd been on his way to mend the roof when suddenly he thought he'd gone too high and seen an angel, which was her ladyship's self.

The last window under the roof was all over stars, not on account of its altitude but because there was hardly an inch of it that wasn't cracked.

Cassidy looked in. He saw, seated at a table, not so much a broth of a boy but more of a stew, as he was on the thick and lumpish side. He was deeply engaged in trying to insert a small ship into a large bottle.

There was a card lying on the table, and Cassidy, by

twisting his head almost off at the neck, was able to read it. Covered all over with hearts and arrows, it said: "FOR MARY."

Cassidy nearly fell with the shock of it. He recovered himself and tapped on the window, and a piece of glass fell out.

The boy looked up and, in his sudden fright, thrust the ship against the neck of the bottle with such force that the ship was instantly destroyed.

Cassidy said through the narrow triangle of air, "If that's for Mary Flatley, I'll trouble ye not to lay eyes on her again and tell her that Cassidy's come!"

The boy stared at the star-crossed face at the window and then at the shipwreck in his hands.

"It was for Mary Harris. And you've broke my window and I'll get the blame."

"So it's another Mary altogether!" cried Cassidy, unable to believe that there were two of them. "Heaven be praised, as we've both had a near escape!"

They stared at each other: the one mournful, though his Mary lived but two streets away, and the other beaming all over his face, though *his* Mary might have been anywhere from Brighton all the way around to Newcastle. Thus the two lovers met in midair.

"And is her hair as black as a raven's wing?" inquired Cassidy professionally, resting his elbow on the sill and cupping his chin in his palm, so that O'Rourke, down below, felt like shaking him off the ladder to remind him that he ought to be going up it.

"It's a sort of brown," said the boy. "I think."

"And are her eyes full of a green fire so bright that

all the world goes dark when she sinks her lashes and puts it out?"

"No," said the boy. "They're a sort of brown, too. With speckles."

"That's a shame!" cried Cassidy. "But maybe she'll be able to see well enough without 'em one day!"

"Speckles," said the boy defensively. "Not spectacles."

A ship's bell clanged somewhere in the house. Four times.

"It's for me," said the boy, and went.

Cassidy examined the room. There were ships' posters all over the walls, advising able-bodied seamen, desirous of sailing to foreign ports, to present themselves aboard at ungodly hours of the morning.

Cassidy saw that all the vessels' names had been scored out and "Mary Harris" written in their place. It seemed that from China to the Cape there was no way to go but under the flag of the lass with the speckled eyes.

"Ah, but he's got it bad!" sighed Cassidy with all the satisfaction of finding a fellow sufferer.

He longed to compare symptoms and exchange pangs, for love is a sickness like any other, save nobody wants to be cured. A great tremble went through him, but this was because O'Rourke had shaken the ladder.

Cassidy went up and peered over the edge of the roof. Sure enough, two slates were gone, and you could see that, at the first breath of a wind strong enough to lift a feather, another dozen would be gone. The batten was halfway to being rotten, and all things considered, a new roof would be cheaper in the long run and twenty pounds well spent.

He came down and told O'Rourke, adding that there was a window broken that might bring in another shilling.

They knocked on the door and put it to the housekeeper, who went away and put it to the master, who put it that Cassidy and O'Rourke were a pair of loafing Irish rogues and five shillings was all they were going to get.

They went out to the cart, and Cassidy said, "It was another Mary, O'Rourke! Would ye believe it?"

O'Rourke nodded and sighed. They returned to the back of the house with rope and tackle and a basket of slates. Cassidy climbed the ladder again and looked in at the window under the roof.

The boy was back and with a friend. The friend was smallish and pale and gave off a strong sense of ink and intelligence. They stared at Cassidy in a state of suspended conversation.

Cassidy raised a finger in salute, and his heart went out to the first boy on whose face was frozen a look of boundless hope and boundless despair.

It was a lover's look if ever Cassidy had seen one, and he'd have given his right arm to have been of any help.

Then he and the ladder shuddered together, and O'Rourke shouted up, "Will ye get a move on, Cassidy, or ye'll be as old as Mary Flatley's grandfather by the time ye get down!"

Chapter Two

THE larger boy—and the room's principal inhabitant—was Bostock. He was thirteen and a half and stood, in a manner of speaking, on the threshold of manhood. In fact, he'd knocked on the door but as yet had received no definite answer.

His visitor was Harris, who, with a look of piercing inquiry, stood right behind him. Bostock wanted to *do;* Harris wanted to *know.*

They were friends and had been through thick and thin together, for which nature seemed to have formed them, Harris being thin and Bostock very thick.

At the present moment, however, their friendship was in the balance, as the Mary Bostock loved was Harris's sister.

Now Harris had several sisters, but unfortunately it seemed that Bostock had picked the most valuable and had nothing comparable to offer in return.

Harris had put it to him fairly, hence Bostock's

boundless despair. Then Harris had made an offer, hence Bostock's boundless hope. Then he'd thought about it, hence the confusion of feeling that was reflected in his face.

They waited for Cassidy to vanish upward, then they resumed their conversation.

"Bosty, old friend," said Harris sincerely, "let me put it to you this way."

Bostock sighed, so Harris pointed out that Bostock, being the only known child of Captain Bostock, retired, was, in law, the heir to all his property.

Bostock agreed.

Harris went on. He didn't mean to suggest that Captain Bostock was in any immediate danger of "going out with the tide," as that sailorly man would have expressed it, but only that he was unlikely to be in full possession of his health and strength for some time to come.

Bostock looked doubtful, but Harris, being the son of Dr. Harris, who was looking after Captain Bostock's gout, and therefore in a position to know what he was talking about, assured Bostock that the captain would be unable to rise from his sick-chair and enjoy his property on the upper floors in the foreseeable future.

Bostock nodded. So far he was with Harris.

Therefore, said Harris, the property had passed, as it were, into the regency of Bostock, as it wasn't to be supposed his ma wanted it. It was in Bostock's gift, which any court in the land would uphold, and Captain Bostock himself, being a Justice of the Peace, would find it hard to deny. Not that Harris advised consulting him, but it was something to bear in mind.

Harris smiled and rested his case.

The property that particularly interested him and had given rise to these ingenious arguments was Captain Bostock's brass telescope. It was kept in a small room at the top of the house, known as the Crow's Nest, and was well beyond Captain Bostock's present range of activity.

Harris's reasons for wanting it were about as lofty as you could get. The heavens themselves. Pigott's comet, which was rushing across the sky at the rate of about an inch a night, foretelling the deaths of kings, the fall of governments, and other national benefits, was predicted to appear at its brightest on Saturday night, April 6. This was in three days' time.

Although the comet could hardly be seen at all and at best would appear as something between a bright pinprick and a flaming pimple, there was to be an outing to the top of Devil's Dyke to view the grandeur of the occasion.

There was to be chicken, veal pies, cheese, wine, and lemonade for the children. Also, if the weather proved kind, there was to be music and dancing. Pigott's comet, which, by the way, was a highly undistinguished object, would have been enchanted if it had known.

Everybody was looking forward to the occasion, and great plans were afoot for going with this or that companion and falling under the comet's romantic spell. In fact, you might have thought it was a kind of speedy Cupid, visiting Brighton for the Easter holidays and showering arrows down on the town.

But not on Harris. While every Jack thought of his

Jill, Harris thought of Captain Bostock's brass telescope.

He'd always wanted it, but until Captain Bostock had been laid low with gout and Bostock had been laid low with love, he'd seen no way of getting it.

Now, however, with the happy onset of the two diseases—the one in Bostock's heart and the other in Captain Bostock's toe—he saw his way clear to realizing his ambition. In exchange for what was almost Bostock's telescope he felt himself able to offer the affections of his sister Mary.

He promised faithfully to advise and assist Bostock to the utmost of his ability and to leave no stone unturned in bringing Mary to heel. He gave him his solemn word that Mary would be his companion for the night of the comet.

Bostock beamed, and Harris shook him by the hand.

"There, Bosty, old friend! I can't say fairer than that! Now just get the telescope."

Bostock's beam faded and was replaced by a look of creeping doubt. He couldn't help feeling that something might go wrong. He didn't know why he should feel like that, with Harris looking so confident; it was just that there was a vague shadow at the back of his mind that worried him. As there wasn't much at the front of it, anything at the back was worrying.

Harris watched him closely. "You do want her, Bosty?"

"Oh, yes, yes!"

"Then get the telescope, old friend."

Bostock fidgeted. He longed to find some way out of

his dilemma without appearing to question Harris's wisdom.

He respected Harris. He admired Harris beyond anybody else in the world. But did not Harris think his case was really hopeless? Mary was such a scornful, slender, acrobatic girl, and she never gave him a second glance unless it was to express twice the disdain she'd shown in her first.

How could Harris, brilliant as he was, have dominion over so wild and free a heart? Surely it was asking too much.

It wasn't.

"I know her, Bosty, old friend," said Harris. "She's my sister, flesh of my flesh and bone of my bone. I know her through and through, like a pane of glass." He smiled dreamily. "We were in the same womb, Bosty," he murmured reminiscently, and Bostock received an indistinct picture of Harris, in a warm dark place, scientifically observing Mary growing more complicated, month by month.

"But—but what if my pa gets better and goes up to the Crow's Nest?" pleaded Bostock, finding another avenue of escape.

"My pa says he'll be lucky to be on his feet by Christmas," said Harris, closing it. "And he's dosing him, so he ought to know."

"But—but after that?"

"Then I'll lend it to you back again," said Harris. "Until it's yours for good."

Bostock thanked him, and then the awful solemnity hinted at by "yours for good" saddened him.

"I think I'll be sorry, you know, when he goes. Out with the tide, I mean."

"It's got to happen to all of them," said Harris, carefully excluding himself. "Someday."

There was a pause in which they both stared at Cassidy's stoutly gaitered feet, shifting on the rung of the ladder. Then Harris, judging that he'd allowed enough time for Bostock to recover from his pa's future death, murmured, "The telescope, old friend."

Bostock said unhappily, "But how are we going to get it out without being seen, Harris?"

Harris pointed to Cassidy's feet.

"But what if my pa sees it going down past his window?"

"I'll go and ask after his toe. That'll take his mind off the window."

"But he said he never wanted to set eyes on you again for as long as he lived, Harris. And my ma says that aggravation only makes him worse."

"Makes him worse?" said Harris with a smile. "Then he won't be up till *after* Christmas, will he! The telescope, old friend!"

"You think of everything, Harris," said Bostock with unwilling admiration.

He left the room and in a little while came back with Harris's heart's desire. It was a sleek and beautiful object, of the brightest brass, that opened and shut like a flexible sunbeam. It had a neat leather cap at either end, like a pair of stoppers for keeping the more stirring sights within.

Somewhere inside its long dark heart, between glass and glass, there must have been a thousand dreaming ships, some becalmed, with sails as limp as Monday shirts, some leaning dangerously into the wind, and some in a kind of nightmare, dashing themselves angrily against rocks, as if to rid themselves of the tiny, itching figures that would not let go and be drowned.

Harris, raptly gazing at it, saw, in addition to Pigott's comet, stars of unimaginable brightness and planets hitherto unknown that would shortly bear a name. He saw Harris Minor, orbiting the sun, and Harris Major, constellated around with a host of lesser lights, among which would be a Moon of Bostock, for friendship's sake.

Cassidy, looping his green length down to pick another slate out of the basket, was also captivated by the splendid instrument. He saw himself sitting on a shoulder of the Downs, raking out all the streets until he saw Mary Flatley, maybe as she shook a sheet out of an upstairs window. And he'd call out, "Cassidy's come!"

Up she'd look, with her bright green eyes, and smile, for sure to God, she'd be near enough to touch, though she was a hundred miles away!

Even Bostock was stirred. He saw himself with Mary Harris, right on the top of Devil's Dyke. He saw Saturday night as if it were here and now, for was it not the business of a telescope to bring what was far away near at hand?

He gave the telescope to Harris and received in exchange the absolute assurance of Mary's heart.

Harris opened the window and asked Cassidy if he would be good enough to take the article to a house, two streets away.

Cassidy, descending to a convenient height, took the instrument, removed the stoppers, and placed it to his eye. A sweeping blur of blue and green communicated itself to him, and then O'Rourke's face, with all its bristles and lugubrious aggravation, came up at him like a cannonball.

Deeply impressed by the nearness of his partner, he gave the instrument back and said it was a wonderful terrible thing, and it would cost a silver sixpence to take it, if Bostock was sure it was his own property, else why wasn't he taking it down by the stairs with his own two hands and out the front door like a Christian?

Harris said that any court in the land would uphold Bostock's rights over the property, so that whether it went out by the window or down by the stairs was of no consequence whatever, and threepence was his last offer.

Cassidy said to Bostock that his friend had the brain of a Jesuit, the way it went around corners in a straight line, and that fivepence was *his* last offer as he had overheads to think of, in the way of O'Rourke and the pony, and that threepence would have meant a penny each, which was insulting to man and beast.

Harris retired to the back of the room and conferred with Bostock.

"Fourpence," he said, coming back.

"Fourpence ha'penny," said Cassidy. "And have ye got it?"

Bostock produced the money—which was all he had —and Cassidy reached.

"On delivery," said Harris. "I'll be waiting."

"He'll end up as Pope," said Cassidy admiringly. "If the Protestants don't get to him first!"

Harris handed over the telescope.

"And which house is it to be?"

"Two streets down that way. You can't miss it. There's a brass plate outside. Dr. Harris."

"Harris, did he say?"

Bostock nodded.

"Not the Harris that belongs with that same Mary with the speckled eyes?"

Bostock nodded again.

"Then why didn't ye tell me in the first place?" cried Cassidy. "I'd have taken the article for nothing and been proud to! But now it's too late. I can't go back on me word. Oh, 'tis the very devil to be an honest man!"

He laid the telescope in the basket.

"May it bring us all our hearts' desires! A Mary for you, and a Mary for me, and health, wealth, and happiness for yer friend!"

Harris vanished, and Bostock watched the basket descend. Suddenly he had the terrible feeling of one who has not only burned his boats but neglected to get off them first. He wanted to call the telescope back, but it was too late. The basket was down, and in a moment Cassidy and his father's property had vanished from sight.

Chapter Three

Cassidy had a terrible fight with the telescope. It kept slithering out from under his arm and standing bolt upright before him, like a brass serpent with a glass eye.

"Cass-ss-idy! Cass-ss-idy! Ye'd get a couple of pounds if ye slipped me to a pawnshop and nobody would be any the wiser!"

"Be silent, ye filthy beast!" cried Cassidy, grasping it around the neck as if he'd strangle it. "I'm an honest man!"

"Cass-ss-idy! Cass-ss-idy! Maybe even two pounds ten?"

"Hold yer tongue, ye brassy snake! Another word and I'll wrap ye 'round a railing and then ye'll not be worth a farthin' of anybody's money!"

So Cassidy fought with the devil all the way, but love had turned him into an angel, so he conquered in the end.

He found Dr. Harris's house without difficulty. He

knew it for a doctor's right away, for beside the tradesman's door was a long stone trough on four carved
paws, looking exactly like a coffin standing in its stock-
inged feet.

Not that Dr. Harris was a bad physician or would
have advertised so plainly even if he had been. He had
bought the trough when an old mansion at the top of
the street had been pulled down to make way for a
row of smart new villas. It was going to have flowers
in it, but in the meantime it was used by butchers'
boys, bakers' boys, and fishmongers' boys, who hid in
it and frightened the wits out of the Harrises' maid by
pretending to be dead.

As Cassidy approached, a hand rose out of the tomb
and beckoned. It was Harris's. He lay in the tomb like
a crusader, among earwigs, beetles, and leaves.

He was very much relieved to see Cassidy as the
thought had crossed his mind, too, that the telescope
would have been worth more than fourpence ha'penny, had Cassidy so desired. Harris had, in fact, been
wondering, if the worse came to the worst and the
telescope vanished from human sight, would he still
be liable for the affections of Mary, or could he return
Bostock's money and call it a day?

But Cassidy had turned up, so he handed over Bostock's money, and Cassidy handed over Captain Bostock's telescope. Bostock himself was not present, as
Harris had told him to smarten himself up, as women,
like moths, were attracted to clothes.

Harris had discovered this, both from personal ob-
servation and from a learned article on Courtship that
he had consulted on Bostock's behalf. It was "The

Courtship of Animals," but Harris did not see that it made any difference, and there was now lodged in his enormous brain a quantity of interesting information which he hoped to put into effect.

"Are ye acquainted with a lass—" began Cassidy, wondering if fate might at last reward him for his honesty and produce Mary Flatley then and there.

There came the sound of the front door opening. Instantly Harris and the telescope sank into obscurity, so Cassidy, raising a finger in salute, strolled back to the street.

He saw that a girl had come out of the Harris front door. She was dressed in pink-and-white spotted muslin and wore an Easter bonnet fit to charm the birds.

It was (or Cassidy was a Dutchman!) the Mary with the speckled eyes! At once he thought of the anguished lover at the window, and he felt an overwhelming desire to be of help. Perhaps, he thought, someone might do the same for him one day.

"And—and is it Miss Harris I'm addressin'?" he asked, hastening to catch up with her, for she went like a wind through a rose garden, all rustles and scent.

He asked to make sure, for God knew what mischief would follow if he got the wrong girl! Cassidy was nobody's fool!

She turned. It was her, all right. She had speckled eyes and her brother's little face, only she'd so improved on it that it was chalk and cheese and you'd not have known if she hadn't come out of the same house and answered to the same name.

"Yes? I'm Miss Harris. What do you want?"

" 'Tis not what I want, me darlin'," he said. "Though

were me heart me own ye should have it directly. I speak for another."

She looked at him in astonishment, then frowned angrily and tried to pass. But Cassidy, hopping backwards in front of her, kept pace and talked so eloquently on another's behalf that even a maid shaking a duster out of an upstairs window of one of the smart new villas could see his white teeth gleaming and his eyes gawping, right through the back of his head.

"I speak for him who's eatin' out his heart for the love of ye," panted Cassidy. "Oh, pity him, me darlin', for he's as fine a young man as ye're likely to meet with this side o' the grave!"

Miss Harris, still frowning so that Cassidy despaired of softening her heart, stepped this way and that, so that she and he seemed engaged in a sprightly springtime dance, she in dainty muslin and Cassidy in hopeless green.

Although she would like to have heard rather more about it, she wasn't going to lower herself in front of all the neighbors by bandying words with a flat-nosed Irish loafer with his syrupy words and treacly smile.

And yet . . . and yet he'd said somebody loved her. It was a good thing to have heard on a Wednesday morning, no matter from whom.

"Take pity on him!" Cassidy pleaded again, and Miss Harris, in spite of herself, racked her brains to discover on whom it was that she should take pity.

Although she wouldn't have admitted it for worlds, nobody sprang readily to mind.

She did not think of Bostock. She never thought of Bostock. And why should she? She was Miss Dorothy

Harris, and she would have died of shame if she'd known that she'd been mistaken for her younger sister Mary.

At last she evaded Cassidy and stalked away, her mind an absolute ferment of young men who, just possibly, might have been madly in love with her.

Cassidy kissed his hand after her back and went off to find O'Rourke, feeling that he'd given love a helping hand.

"In Dublin's fair city, where girls are so pretty," he sang blithely.

"I first set me eyes on sweet Molly Malone!"

The maid at the upstairs window stopped shaking out her duster, and there was a look on her face that would have brought a good deal more than Dublin Castle tumbling down. It was Mary Flatley!

"So it's yerself, Michael Cassidy!" she sobbed. "Down there in the street and smarmin' up to another bit of skirt in front of me very eyes! I'll give ye Molly Malone! Oh, Cassidy, Cassidy! Ye're a philanderin' villain with no heart but an onion, that ye peel and peel and find nothin' but tears! I'll give me heart and hand to the fishmonger's son!" she wept wildly. "For he's as true as ye are false! Though he's an Englishman and as quiet as a mouse and will never talk of raven's wings, nor sing, nor dance, he'll not make me cry, neither. I'll have him today if he asks. And ye've only yer wickedly wheedlin' self to blame!"

She shook her fist after the cheerfully singing Cassidy and then after the back of Dorothy Harris. She dried her eyes on the curtain and slammed down the window so that the glass cracked from side to side.

Chapter Four

DOROTHY Harris walked on toward the heart of the town. She was to meet her friend, Maggie Hemp, in Collier's Chocolate and Coffee Shop and talk about what they would wear for Saturday night on Devil's Dyke. As they were both, for the time being, without lovers, they meant to go together and stroll, laughingly, arm in arm, and watch the goings-on with disinterested amusement, come what may.

She walked quite briskly to begin with, and then fell into a gentle saunter, in which her head drooped, in musing contemplation of the cobbles. Then she looked up and hastened; then she slowed down again.

These changes in her pace reflected changes in her thoughts. That Irishman. What had he meant? She didn't really know what to make of it. Had he been making fun of her? Why should he do such a thing?

Common sense told her she ought to dismiss the whole thing from her mind. If she *did* have an unknown admirer, then surely she'd have known about it by now. And anyway, he wouldn't have left it to an Irish loafer to pass the good news on.

On the other hand, there *were* people who were so agonizingly shy that they ate their hearts out in private and went to their graves without ever opening their hearts to the girls they loved. You read about them—in books.

Yet if a person *was* so agonizingly shy, would he have confided his most sacred feelings to a perfect stranger? It wasn't very likely.

On the other hand (Miss Harris's mind was very full of hands that morning, and they all had a finger in the pie), *someone* had told the Irishman, for how else did he know her name and where to find her? That was a fact, and there was no getting around it, no matter how hard you tried.

So she walked, and so she mused, while the sun struck through her straw bonnet and dappled her face with flying gold—as if to add to her confusion.

"Could it be . . . him?" she wondered, giving way to the Dorothy part of her nature, and fixing on a distant youth who lived in one of the new villas and had once smiled at her absentmindedly. "Could it really be him?"

"No!" answered the Harris portion, which was rather more scientific and not given to flights of fancy. "It couldn't possibly be! He hardly knows you're alive!"

She walked on.

"But what if it's . . . him?" thought Dorothy, loitering again.

"Oh, I hope *not!*" declared the Harris half, shaking the jointly owned head. "I couldn't bear it! What would you say to him? Oh, no! Not *him!*"

She clutched her bonnet strings and hurried on in mock alarm, as if this last, undesirable one were already at her heels.

She slowed down.

"I don't suppose there's any chance that—that it could be . . . *him?*"

The Harris part didn't think so and, what was more, had some sharp words to say on the subject of foolish ambition and making herself a laughingstock. So she hastened on . . . until she found someone else in her Fortunatus's purse of dreams.

A young man driving a gig turned to look at her, either because she was behaving oddly or because there's always something heartwarming about the sight of a girl of fifteen and three-quarters smiling to herself and wearing the spring sunshine as if it had just been made for her.

Not that Dorothy Harris was what you would have called pretty. She wasn't likely to strike anyone all of a heap—unless she walked into him. She was small, like all the Harrises, but she certainly had an odd fascination, especially when she wasn't thinking about it.

She stared after the young man and instantly en rolled him as a suspect.

"Don't be ridiculous!" snapped the Harris in her. "You don't know him from Adam!"

"Oh, don't be such a wet blanket!" said Dorothy. "What ever would have happened to Eve if she'd listened to you!"

27

Collier's Chocolate and Coffee Shop was in Bartholomews, which was the oldest, noisiest, stoniest, fishiest part of the town. Most of the houses looked as if they'd been shrugged down North Street in a heap and were only just picking themselves up.

On Wednesdays, Thursdays, and Fridays, Mr. Collier served coffee or chocolate in delicate gold-edged cups for threepence, with a marzipan fancy for no extra charge.

Everybody went, and there was always a scramble for the best seats, which were in the new bow window that Mr. Collier, who liked to move with the times, had installed.

Maggie Hemp was there already. She beckoned imperiously to Dorothy, indicating through the window that she'd been guarding an empty chair with her life.

Eagerly Dorothy squeezed into Collier's; the doorway was still the old one and as narrow as sin. She joined her friend.

"Maggie!" she panted, sitting down with a flurry of muslin, and full to bursting with her news.

"You're late," said Miss Hemp coldly. She signaled to Mr. Collier, who was perambulating with his tray.

"Oh, Maggie!"

"I'll have one of *those*, Mr. Collier," said Miss Hemp, pointing thoughtfully to a marzipan crocus.

Dorothy bit her lip and picked a daffodil. She'd have picked Mr. Collier's thumb if it had been nearest, she was so impatient to talk.

"Maggie! You'll never guess what—"

"Mr. Collier!" called Miss Hemp, ignoring her.

"Yes, miss?"

"Could we have the sugar, please?"

"It's on the table, miss."

"Oh! Oh, I see."

"Maggie! You'll never guess what—"

"Dolly! Are you sitting on my glove?"

"No, I'm *not*! *Please,* Maggie, let me tell you what happened just now!"

"All right, Dolly," said Maggie Hemp, feeling that she'd punished her friend sufficiently for having been late. *"Now* you can tell me, dear."

So Dorothy, her spirits a little dashed, but reviving quickly, told Maggie about her meeting with the strange Irishman. She told it very amusingly and admitted that it was all probably nonsense and didn't mean anything at all. But wasn't it a strange thing to have happened?

She said it was nonsense not because she believed that it was but because she didn't want to make Maggie, who was rather touchy, jealous. She was rather hoping that they could both laugh and joke about who could possibly be in love with her. It seemed a pleasant subject.

However, as she rambled on, Maggie Hemp couldn't help noticing that Dolly kept staring around the room and even looking over her, Maggie's, shoulder to see who was passing by outside. Not even the burly fishermen who stumped into Saunders' Marine Stores and Fishing Tackle next door and came out in enormous new yellow boots were safe from her promiscuously roving eye.

Miss Hemp began to feel a little neglected. She felt that Dolly wasn't really with her. Also, she couldn't help feeling that, if the Irishman's words turned out to be only half true, then Dolly Harris would drop her like a hot potato, and that would be the end of Saturday night.

"He must have been off his head, Dolly!" said Miss Hemp briskly. "Or drunk, most likely. You know what those Irishmen are!"

"I *did* say it was probably all nonsense," said Dorothy. She was embarrassed to find that her wandering gaze had attracted a small boy, who, tired of gazing at unattainable shrimping nets and bouquets of mackerel knives next door, had come to make goldfish faces at her through the glass.

She blushed and concentrated again on her friend.

"But just for the sake of *supposing,* Maggie, who do you think it could be?"

"I really can't imagine, Dolly."

"But what if it's—"

"Oh, for goodness' sake, don't be so silly!" said Miss Hemp, losing patience. "I thought we were going to talk about Saturday night! We're still going, I suppose? You haven't changed your mind, Dolly?"

"Oh, no, Maggie! I wouldn't do a thing like that!"

"I can always find somebody else," said Miss Hemp warningly.

She was a year older than Dolly and a good deal prettier. She was particularly irritated as she'd felt she was doing Dolly Harris a favor by going with her. She had no intention of playing second fiddle to little Dolly's daydreams.

In fact, the more she thought about it the angrier she became. She believed Dolly had made the whole thing up. There never had been an Irishman . . . still less an unknown admirer. She began to bang her finger rhythmically against the edge of the table.

"I don't know why you're so cross, Maggie."

"I'm not in the least cross, Dolly. Why should *I* be cross with *you,* of all people?"

Dolly bit her lip. She wished she'd never told Maggie about her adventure. Somehow Maggie made it all seem so stupid. She shouldn't have told anybody. She should have kept it to herself. Nobody really understood the way she felt about things, except, possibly, that Mysterious Person, who also kept things to himself. *Who could he be?*

She picked up her cake and stared somewhat gloomily out the window, observing a young woman, in a green shawl and with a basket over her arm, going in to Saunders'.

"You haven't answered me, Dolly."

"I don't see what there is to talk about, Maggie."

"I asked you why you thought I should be cross with you."

"I don't know, Maggie. I really don't know . . . unless it's because you're jealous of what that Irishman told me."

"Jealous?" cried Miss Hemp, setting down her cup with a loud clatter. "*Jealous*? Me, jealous of *you,* Dolly Harris? Really, it's quite the funniest thing I've ever heard!"

She paused to express her merriment by a very ill-natured laugh indeed, and then went on to demolish

31

her friend's pretensions by reminding her that she was hardly of a stature or appearance to drive men wild, and that, if it hadn't been for her—Miss Hemp's —generosity in the way of cast-off admirers, she wouldn't have got closer to a young man than to that stupid Pigott's comet!

Dorothy listened incredulously. She stood up. Her eyes were filled with tears.

"I hate you, Maggie Hemp! I really hate you!"

She left the table, and Miss Hemp, as a Parthian shot, offered, "And, what's more, Dolly Harris, I think you made the whole thing up. Unknown admirers, indeed! Pigs might fly, Dolly Harris, before I'll believe that!"

Blindly Dorothy left the shop and stumbled down the two steps outside. Her heart was in such a turmoil that she scarcely knew whether her adventure had taken place or not. She could only feel, as her one-time friend had pointed out, that she was plain, undersized, and unloved.

"Watch where ye're goin', miss!" cried the girl in the green shawl, coming out of Saunders' and knocking into her. "Oh! So it's yerself," she said, looking into Dorothy's face with angry recognition. "Well, ye can have him for all the good it'll do ye! Marry him today for all I care! And may he break his heart for the love of ye, which would serve him right!"

Dorothy tottered. She gaped. Her thoughts whirled around and around. It had happened again! She'd been told that somebody loved her! It hadn't been a dream, after all!

She looked back to Collier's. Maggie Hemp was

standing in the doorway. She *must* have heard! Dorothy tossed her head. So she'd made it all up, had she? Well! *Somebody* loved her. Somebody *loved* her. Somebody loved *her,* she thought, shifting the emphasis, like a figure in a quadrille, all the way down the line.

She marched away with her head in the air, every bit as high as Pigott's comet, while Mary Flatley stared after her, with eyes as green as unripe apples.

Then a fisherman's lad, in red-knitted cap and huge yellow boots, came out of Saunders' and led her away.

They had gone before Maggie Hemp had recovered herself sufficiently to demand the name of Dolly Harris's secret admirer.

Chapter Five

Miss Hemp remained standing in the doorway of Collier's, her breast heaving, her eyes flashing, her nostrils dilating, and her delicate, white-gloved fingers clenching and unclenching, like stricken blossoms. In addition to these little manifestations of her feelings, her left foot had begun to tap the ground with increasing force. There was no telling what it would all have come to if someone had not asked her to step aside as she was obstructing the entrance to the shop.

She scowled and walked away. She had heard enough—quite enough!—to realize that her friend had cruelly deceived her. Her *friend*—and Miss Hemp's lips curled scornfully over the word—had lied to her, had been deceitful and sly.

"Unknown admirer, indeed!" she muttered. "Oh, *very* unknown, when even a twopenny ha'penny servant girl knows all about him! *That's* a real mystery, that is! That's a *real* surprise! Ha—ha! 'I wonder who it can *be,* Maggie?'" she went on, imitating her friend's voice with bitter exaggeration. "'I really can't *imagine!* Who can have fallen in love with little *me?* Isn't it *strange,* Maggie? Isn't it *wonderful,* Maggie? Isn't it *mysterious,* Maggie? Do you think it could all be on account of the *comet,* Maggie?'"

So Miss Hemp continued, jerking out her feelings, like teeth. Her anger fed on itself and drove tears into her eyes, so that she continually had to brush them aside.

She felt lonely and ill-used. Even though she was neat and pretty enough for young men to turn and look after her, nobody really liked her very much. She was just too honest. She never told lies herself, and if she thought anybody was being sly, she just came right out with it and said so. That was her nature and you could take it or leave it. Most people left it.

"You're a mean, sly beast, Dolly Harris!" she declared as she stalked along East Street.

"But *who could he be?*" she wondered, and she slowed down.

She shook her head and walked on quickly. Then she stopped; then she went on; then she stopped again, much as Dorothy had done, as a wide variety of young men presented themselves to her tortured mind.

"Could it be . . . *him?* Very likely! He's as sly as Dolly! Or . . . *him?* She's welcome to *that* one! But what if it was . . . *him?* Oh, the vile deceitful wretch! How could he? Oh, I hate and despise you all!"

She didn't know whether to be more hurt or angry that Dolly should have kept such a secret from her.

Then she realized all of a sudden that Dolly had done it on purpose to trap her into speaking her mind!

Of course, that was it! Dolly must have known all along that Maggie would never have swallowed that cock-and-bull story about the Irishman! That's why she'd made it up! She'd done it on purpose to *force* poor, unsuspecting Maggie Hemp into a quarrel so she could get rid of her and go off to Devil's Dyke with her sly lover on her own!

"Oh, you nasty little calculating bitch!" cried Maggie Hemp, her fury rising to great heights as she marched across North Street and was nearly knocked down by a cart. "Why couldn't you have come out with it instead of all that lying? Why couldn't you have said openly, 'Maggie dear, do you mind very much if we don't go and watch the comet together? You see, there's somebody else.' Why couldn't you have told the truth, you viper, you? I would have understood. I would have said: 'Of course, Dolly. I don't mind a bit.' But no! Not you, Dolly Harris! You're just like the rest of them, lying and cheating and being sly . . . like—like weasels and stoats and—and other things!"

As Miss Hemp's father was a butcher, it was only natural for her to associate the worst failings in character with animals you couldn't eat.

Poor Maggie Hemp! She never came across a deer or a nice tender lamb; she was always finding herself to be the one honest soul in a nasty sly world. And the worst of it was that when she found people out, they always turned on her in the cruelest way.

"Maggie Hemp!" someone once said to her after she'd told that person that she knew perfectly well what was going on. "You must have a mind like a corkscrew to think in the roundabout, twisted way you do!"

By the time she got home, her eyes were quite swollen from weeping, and the burning question of who was Dolly Harris's secret lover was still unanswered.

It so tormented her that she went straight up to her room and quite forgot her music lesson until her mother came to call her. She was a quarter of an hour late, and her teacher, Mr. Philip Top-Morlion, had become very agitated.

Ordinarily he was a mild young man who taught the flute and fiddle and helped out at dances. But lately his father, Monsieur Maurice Top-Morlion—a Frenchman who had married an English lady—had been laid up with a stomach disorder on account of shellfish, so all the work was loaded onto Philip.

In addition to his own instruments, he now had to teach the cello and the pianoforte to young ladies all over the town. If one pupil was thoughtless enough to be a quarter of an hour late, Philip, with his father's cello strapped to his back, had to run like a hare to his next lesson, as his mother, who taught drawing, singing, and dancing, always wanted the pony and cart.

Consequently he was rather abrupt with Miss Hemp. When he rose to go and she pointed out that she'd had only fifty minutes instead of the hour her pa paid for, he reminded her that she was the one who'd been late, and it wasn't fair to expect Miss Harris to suffer on her account.

"Miss *Harris*? Miss *Dolly* Harris?"

"Yes," said Philip with every appearance of innocence. "My father's ill so I'm giving her her lesson today."

"How very convenient," said Miss Hemp, as everything suddenly became as clear as crystal to her. "How *very* convenient for you, Mr. Top-Morlion!"

"Not really, Miss Hemp. It's quite a long way from here, you know."

"*Quite* a long way," repeated Miss Hemp. "And a very *twisting, roundabout* way, if I might say so."

"I don't understand you, Miss Hemp. It's quite a straight road once you're past North Street."

"*You* might call it a straight road, and *she* might call it a straight road," said Miss Hemp, grasping her flute like a truncheon. "But other people might think differently, Mr. Top-Morlion."

"I—I really don't know what you're talking about, Miss Hemp! Please, I must go now. I can't keep Miss Harris waiting any longer."

"Oh, no! *That* would never do! Don't keep Miss Harris *waiting!*"

"Please practice that last piece before next week."

"Oh, yes. Before *Saturday,* especially. We wouldn't want anything to go wrong before *Saturday,* would we! We must look after poor, silly Miss Hemp until *Saturday,* mustn't we! We must keep her *busy!*" said Miss Hemp, choking back her sobs in a series of moist explosions.

"Go on, Mr. Top-Morlion! Don't keep Miss Harris waiting! Go to her! Run—run, you—you *tomcat,* you!"

Chapter Six

Philip Top-Morlion, always in a hurry, trotted away from the Hemps' with his flute in his pocket, his fiddle under his arm, and his father's cello bumping against his back, where it was fastened by a complicated harness of straps. In addition, he carried an old leather case, so enormously bloated with songs, sonatas, duets, concertos, and the several beginnings of a grand symphony of his own composing that it was in constant danger of exploding and strewing his path with an autumn of tunes.

He was all music. He lived it, he breathed it, and even had dreams of eating it: whole platefuls of crochets the size of mutton chops. The very frown of perplexity that at present furrowed his brow declared itself in five parallel lines, like a stave.

"What the devil was she talking about?" he muttered.

He didn't know Miss Harris from Eve, and all that was happening on the Saturday night was that he and his family had been engaged to play music for dancing on Devil's Dyke if the weather proved kind. So far as he was concerned, Miss Harris and Miss Hemp could go wherever Pigott's comet was going. And the sooner the better.

He disliked all the young ladies to whom he was forced to give lessons, and he disliked their parents even more. He disliked them for the way they patronized music as if it were a mere pastime, and he disliked them for the way they patronized *him*.

True, when he entered a house and divested himself of his instrumental shell—his flute, his fiddle, his father's cello, and his music case—there stood revealed a somewhat threadbare youth, as thin and melancholy as a penny whistle. But there was a soul within him that soared in regions sublime. It ought to have been respected, instead of being received with, "It's only that Mr. Top-Morlion, dear. Now don't tease the poor young man!"

Crash—crash—crash! went horrid discords inside his breast, and huge fortissimos of anger thundered unheard as his maddeningly meek voice inquired, "And have you practiced your last piece, miss?"

Of all his pupils he disliked Miss Hemp the most heartily. He had been teaching her to play the flute for about half a year, and it was only by the greatest effort that he'd refrained from filling her spirit with music by way of thrusting that melodious instrument down her throat as far as it would go.

He detested her so much that he couldn't help thinking that Miss Harris, whatever she was like, must have had some good points, if only because she'd annoyed Miss Hemp.

With this in mind, he reached the Harris residence at about a quarter to four.

"Miss Harris?" he inquired as the maidservant answered his knock.

"Which one?" said she with a look of stupid cunning. "We 'ave four. There's Miss Adelaide, what's one. There's Miss Caroline, what's eight. There's Miss Mary, what's rising fourteen, and there's Miss Dorothy, what'll be sixteen in July. Take your pick."

Somewhat taken aback by the quantity of Miss Harrises available, he frowned, and then supposed it was Miss Dorothy. The maid nodded as if he'd made a wise choice. She went off to announce him while he unharnessed himself and stood in the hall, awaiting the appearance of Miss Hemp's enemy. He couldn't help looking forward to it with interest.

The Harrises were in the dining parlor, sitting uncomfortably around the table. Both the Harrises and the table were in a state of glazed decoration; pudding pies, jam tarts, marzipan fancies, and a large purple wine jelly vied in splendor with the gleaming Harris ladies. They were all awaiting the arrival of Dr. Harris, who was bringing two distinguished colleagues back to tea.

Harris himself had passed the news on, and if anyone doubted him, they might ask Morgan, the Harrises' nurse, who had been present when Dr. Harris had mentioned it.

Unluckily Morgan was out for the day, so Harris's word stood alone and unsupported. Ordinarily it was not an edifice calculated to inspire much confidence, but Mrs. Harris, who creaked awkwardly behind a doctor's ransom of silver and best china, could not, for the life of her, see any reason for her son's having told so stupid a lie. Even for him it would have been quite pointless.

"Are you sure your father said he was coming back at half past three?"

Harris was sure.

She stared hard at her son. He *must* have been telling the truth.

Harris stared unflinchingly back. He had not been telling the truth. It was not Dr. Harris and two distinguished colleagues who were coming to tea. It was Bostock.

Bostock was the important visitor for whom the silver had been polished, the best china set forth, the town ransacked for delicacies, the great wine jelly produced, the Harris ladies squeezed into uncomfortable finery, and three extra places laid. True, Harris might have said one distinguished colleague, but in his experience they usually came in pairs.

The whole splendid occasion was the product of Harris's remarkable brain. Being deeply committed to the disposal of Mary (who, by the way, he would have exchanged for a pair of spectacles, let alone a valuable brass telescope), Harris had devised the present scheme so that Mary would be unable to retire when Bostock arrived.

Usually, when Bosty called, she went off like a

rocket, with a hiss and a giggle and a loud slamming of doors. In such circumstances, all the knowledge Harris had acquired from the learned article on Courtship would have been in vain. Both parties had to be present in order for anything to work. So Harris had arranged it, and now he awaited the appearance of Bostock with the utmost confidence in the learned article from which the scheme had derived.

The door opened.

"Young gentleman for Miss Harris," said the maid.

All the Harris faces, in various stages of age and appetite, turned and lit up, like a row of painted lanterns.

Young gentleman for Miss Harris? Which Miss Harris? But the maid, a bad bargain who cost little and gave less, had gone.

Harris stood up. He had divined that "young gentleman" referred to a Bostock who had smartened himself up beyond recognition. If he didn't get to the door first, somebody else would go and tell Bosty to clear off, as important visitors were expected, and so ruin everything.

"I'll go," he said.

Dorothy Harris also stood up. Her mind, still disturbed by the events of the morning, toyed madly with unknown admirers. Young gentleman for Miss Harris? It was *him*! It must be! He was out there in the hall! Oh, my God!

"Since when are *you* Miss Harris?" she demanded of her brother, her voice shaking.

"I thought she said Master Harris," lied Harris, making for the door at high speed.

"Come back!" commanded his sister, traveling with equal velocity around the other side of the table.

At all costs she had to stop that little beast from poking his nose in and ruining everything. Thus both parties, actuated by the same fear, moved rapidly toward the same point.

Dorothy, having started off with a small advantage in distance, arrived first. Then fortune favored Harris. The delay occasioned by Dorothy's having to open the door enabled him to grasp at the vanishing skirts of his sister's gown.

"It might be for me!" he suggested, to which Dorothy responded by jerking forward with all her might and striking out at her brother with her clenched fist.

Harris, in order to avoid the blow, relinquished his hold. Consequently Dorothy, on a final, violent jerk, flew through the door like an arrow.

"Ah!" she cried, traveling at a tremendous speed toward a dimly perceived figure ahead.

It was *him*! It *was* him!

Her aim was true. She struck home into the startled bosom of Philip Top-Morlion.

Never was there a happier meeting, never a luckier shot. Though she did not know it, Dorothy Harris, with her disheveled hair, her flashing eyes, and her small, oddly attractive face, was looking her very best. Had she strived for hours before her mirror, she could never have achieved quite the same breathless, enchanting abandon, and she made as deep an impression on the young man's heart as she did on his stomach and chest.

"Miss Harris?" he inquired, picking himself up and

assisting the girl to her feet. "Miss Dorothy Harris?"

"Yes, yes! I'm Dorothy Harris!" she said eagerly. "We—we were just going to have tea," she added, as if by way of explanation. The young man couldn't help wondering if it was the custom of the house for Harrises to come out of the parlor like grapeshot, before tea.

One did come. Slowly. It was Harris. He frowned. "Oh," he said, and went back again.

"My brother," muttered Dorothy reluctantly. What a vulgar little boy he was! What must the young man think!

She raised her eyes and couldn't help observing, with a slight pang, that her unknown admirer was rather pale, rather thin, and rather shabby.

To be brutally honest, she would have preferred something a little more eye-catching and calculated to inspire Maggie Hemp with envy. But beggars—and she was a beggar in lovers—can't be choosers, so, with a tiny sigh, she noted with approval that he had that full, strong mouth and those dreamy, sideways-looking eyes that come from playing the flute and reading the music at the same time.

"I called," said he, gesturing toward the cello, "to give you your lesson, Miss Harris."

Instantly fear clutched at her heart. Was it possible he wasn't her unknown admirer, after all?

"But—but I always have Monsieur Top-Morlion!"

"He's my father. I'm Philip."

"But why—"

"Your father's gone to see him," said Philip.

What did he mean? What *could* he mean? Only one

thing. Her father had gone to call on his father to make sure that Philip's intentions were honorable!

What else was she to think after all that had happened to her that day, and with the young man himself standing there and looking at her in a way no young man had ever looked at her before?

The thought even crossed her mind that the two distinguished colleagues her father had said he was bringing back to tea would turn out to be Monsieur Top-Morlion and his son! It was just like her pa to keep things secret and want to surprise her. Dear Pa! Maggie Hemp would go quite *green*!

It never entered her head at all that Monsieur Top-Morlion had made himself sick from overeating and that Dr. Harris had gone to see him as a physician, not a father.

"I think it's shellfish," said Philip.

"Oh, no! A father has to be careful, Mr. Top-Morlion!" said Dorothy, supposing him to have said "selfish," as shellfish didn't make sense.

"I warned him," said Philip.

"You shouldn't have done that!" cried Dorothy, imagining high words between father and son, such as one reads about in books. "Really you shouldn't!"

"Why not?"

She didn't answer. She felt she'd taken a wrong turning somewhere. They smiled at each other in a puzzled sort of way. They shook their heads. It didn't matter. Though they might have been talking *at* cross-purposes, there was nothing cross *in* them at all.

"Will you have your lesson now, Miss Harris?"

"Who is it, Dorothy?" came Mrs. Harris's voice from the parlor.

"It's for me, Mama."

"You haven't answered my question, Dorothy."

"It's Philip Top-Morlion, Mama."

"Who?"

"Philip. Monsieur Top-Morlion's son. He's come to give me my lesson."

"Oh, dear! Can't he come back after tea?"

Philip grew pale. Crash—crash—crash! went the discords in his breast. He prepared to go, never to return.

"No, Mama. He couldn't."

Philip decided to stay.

"Oh, well, I suppose you'd better ask him to sit down to tea with us."

"Will you, Mr. Top-Morlion?"

"Thank you, Miss Harris. I'd like that very much."

"I'd like my lesson more."

"More than tea?"

She smiled. Music, not jam tarts and jelly, was the proper food for love.

They went into the parlor, where another place was laid, and they joined the remaining Harrises to await the arrival of Dr. Harris and two distinguished colleagues, who should have come at half past three.

Suddenly there was a loud and shuddering knock upon the front door. The maid jumped, put on her shoes, smoothed her apron, and went to see who was there.

Chapter Seven

IT was Captain Bostock's best coat with its huge cuffs à la marinière, Captain Bostock's best waistcoat that had anchors embroidered over the pockets, and Captain Bostock's gold-braided hat that had been presented to him by his ship's company on his retirement from the sea.

Inside them all stood Bostock, stiff as a post.

He was, as Captain Bostock himself would have expressed it, all shipshape and Bristol-fashion—that is, if the fashion in Bristol was to wear one's hat an inch below one's eyes, and one's sleeves an inch below one's fingers, so that one looked as if one had lost one's arms and one's sight in the service of one's country.

He doffed his hat, revealing a head that shone like a cannonball and smelled powerfully of violets.

"Oh," said the maid. "It's you. Sorry, but they're expectin' quality. You'd best shove off."

Bostock, who, in the brief journey from his own

house to Harris's, had rescued Mary from crocodiles, pirates, and sinking ships with consummate ease, tottered on the step. He didn't know what to do. Harris had told him to come at half past three, and he'd come. He was a little late, but then the rescuing on the way had taken longer than he'd realized. Harris hadn't told him that anybody else was coming. He felt frightened, and dwindled a little more inside the splendor of his apparel.

"But—but—" he croaked.

There was a frog in his throat. Most likely it was the frog that would a-wooing go.

"All right," said the maid, taking pity on him. "I'll go and tell Master Harris that you're here."

Not thinking it necessary to tell Bostock to wait in the hall, she didn't, so he followed her with doglike fidelity and was actually inside the parlor when Mrs. Harris said irritably:

"For goodness' sake, tell him to go away!"

Bostock panicked, not because of what Mrs. Harris had said—which she always said, anyway—but because of the huge number of people assembled in the parlor waiting for him.

There were hundreds of them! They were all shining like anything, in curls, ribbons, bangles, and necklaces, and they were all staring at him!

He was terrified. Everything was looking at him. The very jam tarts on the table seemed to be regarding him with a united, bloodshot glare, as if to say, "It's Bostock! Ha-ha-ha! Did you ever see such a sight!"

At once a morbid conviction was borne upon him

that there was something peculiar about his appearance. Perhaps he'd forgotten to put on his breeches?
Surreptitiously, and under cover of his father's hat, he
felt for them.

"Why, Bosty, old friend!" said Harris, waving to
him.

Good old Harris! Thank God for Harris!

"What an agreeable surprise!" said Harris. "Lucky
you called, ha-ha! We were just going to have tea!"

What on earth did Harris mean? Bostock's misery
increased. Had he made a mistake and come on the
wrong day? Otherwise, why was he a surprise? He
stared at Harris, appalled. Harris nodded reassuringly.
Dear old Harris!

"I'm sorry I'm late," Bostock said.

"Late?" said Harris, looking at him oddly. "Why
should you think you're late, Bosty, when we weren't
expecting you at all? I can't imagine why you should
say such a thing! Ha-ha!"

What a strange laugh!

"But you said half past three," said Bostock, making
a desperate attempt to refresh his friend's memory.
"For tea. Don't you remember, Harris? It was only
this morning."

Now why had Harris gone so white? And why was
his ma looking at him like that and reaching for the
teapot as if she meant to throw it?

"If," said Harris, watching the teapot carefully, "I
mentioned half past three, Bosty, it was with refer-
ence to my pa coming back with two distinguished
colleagues. I think," he went on, chopping off his
words as if they'd been Bostock's fingers, "that—you

—have—got—hold—of—the—wrong—end—of—the —stick. Ha—ha!"

That laugh again.

Mrs. Harris put down the teapot and said evenly, "But I expect your father will get hold of the *right* end of the stick when he comes home."

What did she mean? What had Harris meant? Bostock felt he was in deep waters. He had the strangest sensation that, somehow, he'd betrayed his friend. He felt more frightened than ever.

"I'll come back later, Harris," he said hoarsely.

"Sit down!" said Harris shrilly, and then, mastering himself, added, "Now you're here, old friend."

Hurriedly he pointed to one of the empty chairs, as the terrified Bostock showed every sign of sitting down right where he was.

Harris blamed himself. He ought to have warned Bostock to keep his mouth shut. It was just that Harris, like God, preferred to move in mysterious ways. He'd wanted to amaze Bostock with what he, Harris, could accomplish when he really set his mind to it.

He watched as Bostock crossed the room with the general air of one who expects at any moment to fall down in a fit.

"Here, Bosty. Next to me."

Bostock sat, and Harris, dismissing any future unpleasantness from his mind, waited for the learned article on Courtship to take effect.

Courtship in nature, it had explained, was to be observed in the performance, by the male of the species, of those interesting actions that were ingeniously arranged to arouse in the female a willingness to accept him as a mate. Among such actions perhaps the most striking was the display of bright plumage and the discharge of perfume or scent.

Well, it was done. There was Bosty, got up like a dog's dinner and whiffing like one o'clock. And there was Mary, sitting opposite and at point-blank range. Harris didn't see how Bostock could fail to strike.

"Pooh!" said Mary, waving her hand in front of her nose, as a powerful discharge of perfume from Bostock's hair oil reached her. "What a stink!"

Harris, satisfied that Bostock had struck, punched him violently in the ribs to indicate that he should take advantage of the impression he'd made by engaging Mary in animated conversation. Otherwise, whatever it was he'd aroused would subside again.

Bostock opened his mouth, but nothing came out. Harris kicked him under the table. Bostock moaned. Harris trod on his foot, and Bostock smiled feebly. It was hopeless.

If only Harris had brought a raging lion into the parlor, Bostock would have snatched Mary from its jaws. If only Harris had set fire to the house, Bostock would have saved Mary from the flames. But animated conversation was utterly beyond him.

He was just too modest. In his heart of hearts he couldn't believe that he was worthy of anyone's interest, or that he was anything other than dull, clumsy, and unattractive to behold. And, to be honest, nothing had ever happened to him to make him change his mind.

He sat, paralyzed by the presence of his beloved, who was almost within touching distance, in her best white dress with green ribbons in her hair. From time to time, when nobody was looking, she put out her tongue at him with the rapidity of an angry serpent. Apart from this, she took no notice of him at all.

Harris began to get angry. He'd gone to considerable trouble to put Mary in the way of Bostock, and, what was more, his family had gone to considerable trouble, too. Now it was all being thrown away. A glance at his mother confirmed that she felt the same . . . perhaps even more strongly than he did himself. Fortunately, however, the music teacher had stayed to tea so Harris was safe, as his ma never blew up in company.

Harris stuck a fork into Bostock to draw his attention to the music teacher, who was setting an example Bostock might well have followed, in the way of animated conversation.

Philip Top-Morlion hadn't stopped talking once, and Dorothy, who was sitting next to him, was hanging on to his every word.

More than ever she was convinced he was her unknown admirer, and she wished with all her heart he'd stop talking about music for long enough to ask her to go with him to Devil's Dyke on Saturday night.

In vain she plied him with jam tarts and pudding pies and asked him slyly if he cared about comets or stars. He only smiled his sideways smile and went on about Bach, Handel, and Bononcini until she could have screamed.

Everybody was eating now, as it was plain Dr. Harris wasn't coming, and all the good things dwindled away. Presently nothing remained of the feast but a plate of tarts next to Bostock—who hadn't opened his mouth either to let anything out or to put anything in —and the great wine jelly in its silver dish.

It was an exceptionally fine and costly jelly, full of claret and brandy and all manner of outrageous things. It had been prepared for the outing to Devil's Dyke and would have done Mrs. Harris great credit if only it had been spared.

But it was going to be spared. Mrs. Harris had made up her mind. She would have taken it off the table at once if Monsieur Top-Morlion's son hadn't been present; as it was, she sat and watched the jelly with an attention beside which the stare of a hawk was but a casual glance.

At the smallest motion in its direction, she frowned menacingly and shook her head. It was not going to be touched.

All right! she thought: he (she could not bring herself to mention her son's name) had turned the household upside down. He had caused her to drag herself and her daughters into their uncomfortable best gowns. In addition, he was responsible for her having spent a fortune on cakes and then had had the impudence to invite his idiot friend who was sitting there, stinking the house out with his horrible hair oil.

But that was enough. There had to be a limit. And that limit was the wine jelly. IT WAS NOT GOING TO BE TOUCHED.

Bostock was feeling a little easier. He was sorry that he'd let Harris down, but there it was: you might bring a Bostock to the tea table, but you couldn't make him talk; any more than a horse. It was a pity there hadn't been a lion or a fire. *Then* Harris would have been proud of him!

He gazed achingly at Mary. She wasn't looking at him. Maybe she was thinking about him?

She wasn't. She was thinking about the last plate of jam tarts. She reached toward them.

I'll help her! thought Bostock gallantly. Harris will be pleased!

He also reached toward the dish. Mary, not wanting to be forestalled, hissed warningly. With bewildering rapidity she snatched the tarts away, so that Bostock, taken by surprise, continued after the dish for a short distance. Then he uttered a faint cry and withdrew his arm to its former position. After which he made no further movement and seemed to have stopped breathing.

He was dying. His sleeve was full of blood. He did not know what had happened. He felt no pain and wondered if his heart had burst.

He wanted to die quietly, sitting at the table next to Harris, and with Mary looking on. His dearest friends. He did not want any fuss. He wondered if he ought to apologize to Mrs. Harris. She was certainly looking very angry. Why was she looking so angry? What was she staring at?

Oh! The jelly. Now that was strange. There was the dish, but where was the jelly? It had been there a moment ago. What had become of it?

Bostock thought, which is to say, he knitted his brows and hoped the rest would follow. It did. He was not dying. His sleeve was not full of blood; it was full of jelly. He had scooped it up in his father's enormous cuff à la marinière.

One problem solved, another presented itself. Why wasn't he dying? He wanted to die. If possible, yesterday. He could see no other satisfactory conclusion to the afternoon.

He sat in abject misery, a prey to thoughts of self-destruction, and attempting, by a series of fitful jerks, to persuade the huge, clammy jelly to slide out of his father's cuff and into his father's hat.

At the other end of the table Mrs. Harris stared at him with incredulous loathing, while beside her, as if nothing had happened, Philip Top-Morlion still talked of Bach, Handel, and Bononcini, and Dorothy tried to put in a good word for the stars.

Then Dr. Harris himself came in, and Dorothy couldn't help being mildly disappointed that Philip's father wasn't by his side.

The doctor, seeing Philip, greeted him affably.

"I've just seen your father," he said.

Dorothy's heart began to dance. She could hardly wait for the next words. Would they be, "He has given you his blessing, my boy," as she'd so often read in books? Involuntarily she reached for Philip's hand under the table and squeezed it. Philip looked surprised but squeezed back.

"It was the shellfish all right," said Dr. Harris.

Dorothy let go of Philip's hand.

"I've given him some medicine," went on the doctor pitilessly. "But I'm afraid you'll be troubled with his pupils for a day or two longer yet."

Dorothy stood up. Her face was crimson with shame and embarrassment.

"Your lesson," said Philip. "Will you have it now?"

"I've had it!" sobbed Dorothy. "I've learned my lesson once and for all!"

She fled from the room and rushed upstairs, wishing with all her heart that she was dead, while Bostock and Harris, taking advantage of the confused situation, vanished like ghosts.

Chapter Eight

Harris comforted Bostock. He walked the streets with him, trudged along the beach with him, and went back home with him, where he stayed until Bostock was almost asleep.

Having departed at high speed from the tea table, Harris was in no hurry to return, being anxious to give Time, the Great Healer, every opportunity of acting on his behalf.

Also he was really worried about Bostock, who looked so miserable that Harris feared he'd give up all hopes of Mary and want the telescope back.

"Bosty, old friend," he said gently, as Bostock sat on his bed and mournfully contemplated the ruin of his father's best coat and hat, "trust me."

Bostock looked up. "It's no good, Harris. She doesn't like me."

Harris smiled. "How little you understand these things, Bosty."

"I know when somebody can't stand me!" said Bostock with a flicker of irritation.

Harris dismissed this and explained that the ingenious process of Courtship pursued its course regardless of personal feelings. He, Harris, had studied the matter and knew what he was talking about.

Bostock had really done rather well. Having displayed himself in bright plumage and discharged scent, he had made a definite impression on Mary.

Bostock agreed but felt it hadn't been a very good one. Harris laughed triumphantly. That was exactly as it should have been!

Did Bostock not know that the female always responded to the beginning of Courtship with a display of hostility? Had Bostock not seen the peahen dart out her beak like a dagger, the bitch bare her teeth, the vixen snarl, the mare kick, and even the docile cow heave and moo?

So it had been with Mary. It was the female's way of displaying her independence before subduing herself to the male of her choice. Which, in this case, was Bostock.

If Mary had smiled at him, then he, Harris, would have been doubtful. If she had held his hand, then Harris would have feared that all was lost. But to have her respond with the venomous dislike they had both witnessed filled Harris with confidence.

"Tell me this, Bosty," said Harris, pressing home point after point as if he were pinning down a butterfly. "Was she worse than usual?"

"I think so, Harris. Yes. Now you come to mention it, I think she was."

"Then that proves it, old friend! Don't you see, Bosty? The ritual of Courtship has begun! There's no stopping it now, Bosty, no stopping it at all!"

They shook hands and Harris went home. Bostock was happy again, and so was Harris. He was glad to have restored the admiration of his friend.

Curiously enough, this admiration was as important to Harris as the telescope itself. Although the telescope might have revealed the wonders of the heavens, Bostock revealed the wonders of Harris. Without Bostock, Harris dwelt in darkness, a dead star, a lonely, unconsidered thing.

The house was quiet. Time, the Great Healer, had acted on Harris's behalf, and everyone was asleep. He climbed in through the scullery window and went upstairs.

He heard, in passing, his sister Dorothy sobbing in her sleep. Time had healed nothing for her, and over and over again she relived in her dreams her humiliating mistake about the music teacher's son.

"Oh, no—no—no!" she moaned.

Harris frowned. There was always a female crying somewhere in the house.

He mounted the last flight of stairs and entered his room, which, like himself, was somewhat removed from the rest of the world.

It was a remote, squeezed-under-the-roof Pythagoras of a room, containing one right angle and a great many wrong ones. Wherever you looked, it was impossible not to propose a theorem, and equally impossible to solve it. Even in the darkness there was a sense of immense problems and immense solutions.

Harris sat on his bed and considered the whole question of Courtship. In addition to the display of bright plumage and the discharge of scent, the learned article had described the clashing of beaks and pursuit, music, both vocal and instrumental, and the performing of dances or other antics. There was the presentation of prey or of incdible but otherwise stimulating objects, and, as a footnote, there was noted the curious behavior of the snipe, which plummeted down at a great speed while uttering hoarse cries.

Harris shivered, not at the thought of Bostock plummeting, but because there was a draft. It was blowing through a hole in the window that had been brought about by Harris's having accidentally poked the end of Captain Bostock's telescope through the glass.

The instrument itself lay on the windowsill, gleaming faintly, as if with a mysterious light of its own. Harris gazed at it thoughtfully.

Might not the telescope, which brought the heavens nearer, bring other things nearer, too? Might it not reveal the secrets of *human* courtship?

He went to the window and opened it, and looked out into the night. It was dark, very dark. Somewhere aloft, under a blanket of cloud, Pigott's comet pursued its frantic course; otherwise there were dark houses, dark trees, and a long dark shoulder of the downs, making a landscape of ink. To the north, on top of Dyke Hill, rose St. Nicholas's Church. Both were as black as sin.

Harris set the telescope to his eye. Instantly chimneys, roofs, and the tops of trees swept past in a dark hurry, as if anxious not to be seen.

He thought he saw an owl, with something in its beak, winging its way back to its nest, but he could not be sure. He studied windows, doorways, and the quiet corners of streets. Nothing. Human beings, it seemed, were more secret than the night itself.

Then suddenly a light flickered. It was no more than a tiny yellow pinprick, but in the wide darkness it was an explosion of interest, like a gold tooth in a pirate's beard.

He lost it, then he found it again. It was by the church. It was moving so that every now and then it vanished behind bushes, emitting no more than a fragile sprinkling of yellow, like the pricking of buds.

He put down the telescope rather quickly, as if the distant object of his scrutiny might have turned and seen Harris's eye, suspended in the night.

It was a courting couple all right, performing their mysterious antics in St. Nicholas's churchyard, far from prying eyes.

Harris left his room in great excitement, intending to observe, as closely as he could, an actual human courtship, so that he might put his knowledge at the service of his friend.

He hastened down the stairs, left the house, and sped through the night. He was desperately anxious not to be too late and miss the whole thing.

Not until he was three quarters of the way up Dyke Hill and approaching the churchyard itself did the possibility of his having been mistaken occur to him.

Trees whispered, tombstones loomed, and monuments glared. Harris faltered. He listened in vain for the murmur of lovers' voices and the music of amorous sighs. Regretfully he abandoned the idea of a courting couple and considered instead the possibility of grave robbers, body snatchers, murderers, and other likely inhabitants of a churchyard by night.

He could still see the light, moving about in a thoroughly spectral fashion, and he could hear the slow, heavy thump of mysterious feet.

Harris felt a strong desire to be back in his room, with his head under the blankets, and asleep.

The light drew near, and a long black shadow fell across a grave. Harris, mentally bequeathing his possessions to Bostock and his murdered body to science, moaned and went horribly white.

"Holy Mother of God!" shrieked O'Rourke, coming out from behind a bush and beholding the apparition of Harris. " 'Tis a murdered boy!"

Indeed, it was a ghastly, spectral Harris, whose corpse-like pallor would have deceived any body snatcher into taking him into stock at once.

They both stood, trembling violently and glaring at each other and inspiring as much terror as they felt.

O'Rourke crossed himself and required Harris, in the name of St. Patrick, to vanish and return to those mysterious regions whence he'd come.

Harris would willingly have obliged, but was unable to do so. Paralyzed with dread, he remained motionless in O'Rourke's lantern light.

Then O'Rourke perceived that the terrible, white-faced thing was the friend of the magistrate's son, and Harris perceived that the huge gaunt figure with the lantern was one of the Irish roofers he'd seen at Bostock's house.

"Wh-what are you doing here?" inquired Harris in a tone of voice that suggested that, if O'Rourke didn't choose to say, then he, Harris, would not press the point.

But O'Rourke was so relieved to discover that Harris was flesh and blood—although, by the look of him, there wasn't all that much blood about—that he was only too thankful to talk.

"I was lookin' for somebody," he said, casting his light around the graves. "And I pray to God that I won't be lucky enough to find her."

"Somebody dead?"

"Now would I be lookin' for a livin' lass with her name on a stone and her pretty self under it?"

"Then she is dead!"

"Never say such a thing! If Cassidy heard ye, he'd go right out of his mind! Just say she's somewhere, that's all. And may Cassidy be the first to find her, though he'll fall off his ladder and break his neck!"

O'Rourke beckoned. "Come over here and sit with me on this stone, young sir, and I'll tell ye a tale of love and courtin' that'll bring the tears to yer eyes, even though ye're as small as a wink in a blind man's cup!"

He held out his hand as if to assist the uncertain boy. "I'll tell ye of Cassidy and sweet Mary Flatley, that's been gone for a year and a day. But I tell a lie, for it's tomorrow already, so it'll be a year and two days. 'Twas in Dublin's fair city, and she in the fish business like Molly Malone before her, and Cassidy comin' up to mend the thatch of her father's roof. . . ."

So they sat on the tombstone with the lantern between them, which turned the black midnight yews into a golden bower, while O'Rourke told sadly of Cassidy's courting and Cassidy's seeking and Cassidy's singing under every window, down every street in the land.

Then his face grew longer and even more lugubrious as he told of his own quiet searching down streets of a different kind, where the houses had no windows, and were dwellings for only one.

"But she's in one or the other, and that's for certain-sure, and whichever way it is, no good will come of it, for it'll break Cassidy's heart or break Cassidy's neck."

He put out his lantern, and the trees, the stones, the church, and they themselves sank back, like dreams, into the darkness of the night.

Harris went back to his home, and O'Rourke went back to the King's Head, a little public house in The Lanes, where he and Cassidy shared a room.

"She wasn't there, Cassidy!" he whispered, bending over his sleeping friend. "She wasn't there at all, so ye can still be an honest man!"

Chapter Nine

O'ROURKE shook the end of Cassidy's bed so that Cassidy came out of his dreams with a great start, or, rather, a great stop, which was what O'Rourke had put to them.

" 'Tis tomorrow!" he shouted. "Ye loafin' great bundle of sleep!"

"Where am I?" inquired Cassidy in a grumbling kind of fright.

"In the King's Head!"

"And what monarch might that be with a thought like Michael Cassidy inside of him?"

" 'Tis the public house, ye mad thing—" began O'-Rourke, when he saw that Cassidy was deceiving him, so he went on to inform him that half the world was up and about its business and, most likely, taking the bread from their mouths.

"Another minute!" sighed Cassidy, brightening up his eyes with his knuckles. "Only another minute and she'd have been in me arms! Ye're a hard man, O'-Rourke."

He began to array himself for the day's work, taking particular care with the scraping of his whiskers and the whitening of his teeth, which he polished, first with his tongue and then with a bit of old rag.

"Do I look all right, O'Rourke? D'ye think she'll have me?"

"Ye look fine, Cassidy! Handsome enough to lead a parade!"

"Today's the day, O'Rourke! Today's the day I'll find her! I feel it in me bones!"

O'Rourke nodded. He did not have the heart to remind Cassidy that he'd felt it in his bones every single morning since they'd landed in Liverpool, and it was a marvel that Cassidy could still stand upright, with bones inside of him that told such terrible lies.

They left the King's Head and went down into Bartholomews, where O'Rourke collected a pane of glass from a glazier's, and came back all sideways, like an Irishman in an Egyptian picture, carrying nothing at all.

They went to the stables and Cassidy said they ought to take the pony to the doctor's, as he looked sick as a dog.

"D'ye really think so, Cassidy? For it'll cost us money!"

"Just look at him, O'Rourke! Did ye ever see such a poor beast with so many spots behind his eyes?"

Gloomily, for O'Rourke was no joker and Cassidy always caught him out, he gave Cassidy the glass and the pair of them got up onto the cart.

Then O'Rourke jerked the reins, and Cassidy began to sing, pausing only to pay his high-flown compliments to every pretty girl they passed. Nor did he overlook the plain ones, for Cassidy found something to be charmed by everywhere.

"In Dublin's fair city, where girls are so pretty . . . Good mornin' to yer ladyship! And what might ye be doin' so far from Dublin with such cherries in yer cheeks?

"I first set me eyes on sweet Molly Malone! . . . Oh, but if I'd seen ye first, me darlin', I'd have had no eyes for that Molly Malone! Chalk and cheese! Chalk and cheese!"

So he went on, singing and saluting, and sometimes holding up the glass at a girl as if she were a picture, crying out for a frame, while O'Rourke boomed steadily, "Tiles and slates! Chairs to mend! Pots, kettles, and pans!"

At last they came to the row of smart new villas that sparkled in the sun. "There's the house!" cried O'-Rourke, pointing to the end of the row. " 'Tis a window upstairs in the front!"

He'd spied the cracked glass on the previous day and obtained the business of mending it from the lady of the house herself. They halted.

"And while ye're up there, Cassidy, ye might take a look at the roof and see if ye can wheedle a slate or two down, for she's not a lady to begrudge a shillin'," said O'Rourke.

"That wouldn't befit an honest man," said Cassidy, climbing down.

"For God's sake, Cassidy, it's business and there's nothin' personal in it at all!"

Cassidy beamed.

"She died of a faver, and no one could save her," he sang, carrying the ladder to the front of the house.

"Must ye sing, Cassidy? 'Tis a respectable house!"

"I must, O'Rourke. I must!" said Cassidy, and went on with, "And that was the end of sweet Molly Malone!" so that O'Rourke couldn't help feeling that it would have been a good thing all around.

"Her ghost wheels her barrow, through streets broad and narrow,

"Crying: Cockles and mussels, alive, alive-o!"

He laid the ladder against the wall.

"Alive, alive-o!"

"Go easy, Cassidy, or it's the dead ye'll be awakening with that great bellow!"

"And haven't they been sleepin' long enough, O'-Rourke?" demanded Cassidy, and went on trumpeting his song at the top of his voice.

He began to mount the ladder.

"Alive, alive-o!"

He's like a bird! thought O'Rourke with unwilling admiration, as the smart buttons on the back of Cassidy's green coat winked and twinkled down on him.

Cassidy went dancing up, alive and alive-o-ing all the way. He reached the cracked window and tapped on the glass.

"Alive, alive-o!"

The window flew up.

"Alive, alive- OOOOH!" shrieked Cassidy as Mary Flatley herself looked out.

Like a bird! thought O'Rourke, as down plummeted Cassidy with a hoarse cry.

"Dead!" howled O'Rourke. "Cassidy, are ye dead?"

"Not dead! *Not* dead!" screamed Mary Flatley, coming out of the window almost far enough to follow after. "Don't say ye're dead, Michael Cassidy! Never say that in me hearin'!"

"So it's yerself!" wailed O'Rourke, staring up at the cause of the disaster. "And didn't I always tell him ye'd break his heart or his neck?"

Cassidy lay among bushes, green as a giant leaf, with a face on him as white as any blossom—and him just singing, "Alive, alive-o!"

"Oh, Cassidy, Cassidy! Tell me ye're not dead!"

Never a word out of him, never a look. His eyes lay under lids as quiet as stones.

"Oh, Michael Cassidy, Michael Cassidy!" wept Mary Flatley, coming out of the front door and joining O'-Rourke in his lamentations. "I'll not wed another if only ye'll tell me ye're not dead! For what should I be doin' in this old world without ye?"

The mistress of the house appeared, then neighbors came, and presently there was a little crowd gazing down on the fallen Cassidy and wondering what to do.

Then somebody remembered that a doctor lived nearby, and ran off to fetch him, while Mary Flatley wept and picked leaves and twigs from out of Cassidy's curly black hair.

Dr. Harris came and everybody made way for him. He looked up at the window and down at the ground, for all the world as if he expected to find Cassidy somewhere between. Then Mary Flatley showed him where Cassidy was, and he looked at Cassidy and felt him and listened to him through his green coat and right down to his heart. Then he said that Cassidy was alive and that his neck was as good as yours or mine.

" 'Tis a miracle!" said O'Rourke.

" 'Tis Michael Cassidy!" said Mary Flatley. "And that's miracle enough for me!"

Then O'Rourke took one end of him and two of the villa people took the other, and between them they eased him off the bushes, and Mary Flatley picked up a silver sixpence that had fallen from his pocket and tucked it into his shirt.

They laid him on his ladder and carried him out to the cart, and the lady of the villa said she'd pay the doctor's fee as poor Cassidy had fallen in her service, in a manner of speaking. And Dr. Harris said no, not at all, she wasn't to think of it, as he'd only acted out of common humanity. And O'Rourke, who was all for saving money, agreed that there never was such a common piece of humanity as Michael Cassidy, God bless him!

"He'll need liniment," said Dr. Harris to O'Rourke. "Can you fetch it for him?"

But before O'Rourke could answer, the lady of the villa, anxious to be of service, said she'd send her very own maid.

"We're livin' in the King's Head," said O'Rourke. "The establishment in The Lanes."

"I'll be there before ye!" cried Mary Flatley, and flew back into the villa to put on her best dress and fill a basket, so that Cassidy, when he woke up, should have something good to look at, as well as good to eat.

They put him in the back of the cart where he lay like a fallen knight collected for burial. Sorrowful O'-Rourke briefly turned his countenance—to make sure Cassidy hadn't tumbled off—and the cart trundled away. It was a scene of ancient chivalry, bright as a tear and a thousand years old.

Chapter Ten

HARRIS saw it all. Leaning out of his window like an angel on a bracket, that had, for reasons of short-sightedness, been equipped with a telescope, he had watched Cassidy go climbing up his ladder, singing at every rung.

He had seen the girl come swiftly to her window, her face all wild with longing as she heard her lover's song. And then, just as O'Rourke had predicted in the churchyard, down had plummeted Cassidy with a hoarse cry, remarkably like the snipe.

Harris had witnessed the courting of Cassidy and Mary Flatley, and he could hardly believe his luck.

He had seen everything he needed to know, hanging in a miraculous bubble of light, suspended before his eye.

Fascinated, he observed the girl fly out of the house and rush to Cassidy's side, kneeling and weeping all over him, as if to water him back to life.

Quietly he put the telescope by. The problem was

solved. What had moved one Mary could hardly fail to move another. Courtship, love, and the very springs of passion were, to Harris, now an open book.

He left his room and went downstairs, passing on his way his sister Dorothy, to whom, unhappily, courtship was a book that had been slammed shut. She sniveled, dabbed her swollen eyes, and stared at her brother as if, somehow, he were the author of all her misfortunes.

He departed from the house and went around to the side. He looked into the stone coffin, but Bostock wasn't there, so he went down to the beach.

On the other side of the road Philip Top-Morlion was hanging about, trying to summon up courage to call on Miss Harris and propose another time for her lesson. He was still bewildered by her tempestuous departure from the tea table, particularly after she'd held his hand. He saw Harris and waved.

Harris ignored him. He had a great deal on his mind. Bostock was sitting on a breakwater, hurling stones with tremendous force into the sea, as if to provoke it. But it lay, flat as Sunday, scarcely bothering to lap at the pebbles before drawing itself back with a noise like soup.

The friends shook hands, and Harris perched himself on the breakwater by Bostock's side. Philip Top-Morlion, who'd tottered after, watched from a distance and wondered if he should ask Harris if he thought his sister would like her lesson now.

The two boys appeared to be deep in conversation, and of a very private kind. They kept looking up at the wheeling, shrieking seagulls as if fearing they were eavesdropping on the secrets that each was confiding to the other.

Philip smiled indulgently. What secrets could they have at their age, when their hearts were still sleeping and they knew nothing of the pangs of wounded pride?

He eased his various musical burdens and waited for a suitable moment to approach the two boys. Although he felt that the presence of a grown-up person like himself would probably be flattering, he was sensitive enough not to want to interrupt.

Her brother appeared to be doing most of the talking. He was waving his arms about earnestly, and every now and then he laid a hand on his friend's shoulder with an affectionate, reassuring air.

Presently Bostock stopped throwing stones and began to nod, as if he'd been talked into something. Then, to Philip's surprise, Harris started to sing. It was uncanny, as if there were a bird somewhere inside him that had cut its foot on something sharp.

Philip, the musician, winced, but Philip, the music teacher, felt that the suitable moment had arrived.

He crossed the road and stumbled bulkily over the pebbles of the beach.

"You should take lessons," he said, as if Harris's singing, though pleasing in an artless way, would have benefited tremendously from paid tuition.

Harris looked mildly affronted.

"I think you have talent," lied Philip, not wanting to make an enemy of Miss Harris's brother.

Harris nodded, and Bostock did not look surprised.

"I was wondering," said Philip, "if your sister Dorothy would like her cello lesson this morning."

"It's Thursday," said Harris. "She goes to Collier's. Free cakes."

"Ah, well," said Philip casually, "perhaps another time. Collier's, did you say? I might even see her there."

Harris looked at him carefully. "You won't get in, you know," he said.

Philip Top-Morlion stepped back as if he'd been struck. His eyes filled with tears.

"Thank you," he said shakenly. "Thank you very much!"

He'd never been so insulted in all his life! To be told by a child—a sordid, vulgar, hateful boy!—that he wasn't good enough to be admitted to that cheap little coffee shop in Bartholomews! And after he'd told the boy he had talent!

Philip Top-Morlion raged hopelessly against the injustice of it. Why hadn't he struck the boy? Why hadn't he punched him in the face? Why was he always so sickeningly meek when everywhere you saw stupid arrogance honored? When every loud-mouthed fool was hailed as a genius because he said he was!

Why did he never tell the parents of his simpering pupils what he *really* thought of them? Why did he always say, "Thank you," when he meant, "Damn you!"?

He longed with all his heart to be able to explode with outrage and spread a peacock's tail of anger across the sky. He longed to strut, to give grand concerts and be greeted with reverence and wild applause.

Above all, he longed to see Miss Harris again. She, at least, understood him, and she loved music.

He went down to Bartholomews. He couldn't help himself. It was almost as if he *wanted* to be humiliated. People like Philip Top-Morlion—sensitive, artistic souls—seem to have a passion for exposing themselves to anguish. It's as if only by suffering can they create the masterpieces that give the heedless world its joy.

So Philip Top-Morlion tried to fix his mind on a poignant passage in his grand symphony as he walked past Collier's with knitted brows.

She was there! She was sitting in the window, talking to Miss Hemp. He retraced his steps. Miss Hemp saw him first. She would! She nodded slightly and compressed her lips, as if to say, "You won't get in here, you know."

He smiled, as if to say, "Thank you. Thank you very much."

She said something to Miss Harris. He walked on slowly. He looked back. Miss Harris was staring at him. She was smiling and beckoning!

"Good morning, Mr. Top Morlion," she was mouthing through the glass.

He walked back.

"Good morning, Miss Harris."

"What did you say?"

"I said good morning."

"I can't hear you! Why don't you come inside?"

"I—I—"

"Please!"

"All right. Just for a minute!"

"What?"

"I said—oh, never mind!"

He vanished, and Dorothy looked expectantly toward the edge of the curtain that screened the bow window from the door.

After her terrible night of tears she'd decided to try to make things up with Maggie Hemp before it was too late to go with her to Devil's Dyke. She hated herself for doing it, but there was so little time left and nothing else in view. Now, however, things changed.

"I don't know why you asked him in!" said Miss Hemp with the beginnings of irritation.

"I wanted to ask him about my lesson, Maggie. That's all, really."

She continued to look toward the curtain.

"I wonder what's happened to him?"

"I expect he's changed his mind. You know what men are!"

"He said he was coming . . . just for a minute."

"I thought you said you couldn't hear a word!"

"I'll just go and see where he is!"

"Really, Dolly! You're man mad!"

"I'm not!" said Dolly, fidgeting out of her chair. "Really I'm not! I won't be a minute, Maggie!"

She left the table and whisked around the curtain.

Ah! He *had* come in! Or mostly in. He was standing in the doorway and looking rather flushed.

"Won't you join us, Mr. Top-Morlion?"

He shook his head.

"Why not?"

"I can't."

He tried to smile but felt more like crying. He was the victim of a peculiarly unfortunate circumstance. His father's cello had become wedged in the narrow doorway, and he was strapped to it as firmly as to a stake. The boy Harris had been right. He couldn't get in to Collier's, and, what was worse, he couldn't get out, either.

"Let me help you," said Dorothy, trying not to laugh.

"It ought to be the other way around," said Philip wretchedly. "I mean, isn't it the knight who's supposed to free the lady?"

Back at the table, Miss Hemp began to breathe heavily and to tap her foot. What were they doing? She took Dolly's cake and ate it. What were they talking about? She stared toward the curtain and could just see the edge of Dolly's dress.

If it was only Dolly's lesson, why were they being so secretive about it? She leaned over as far as she could and strained her ears.

Collier's was very noisy. Everybody was clattering cups and talking at once. Nevertheless, over and above it all, Maggie Hemp heard quite distinctly the sound of laughter. His and hers. What were they laughing at?

Her face grew red and her eyes filled up with tears. They were laughing at *her*!

It was as plain as anything. *That's* why they hadn't come back to the table! They wanted to have a good laugh together over silly, honest Maggie Hemp! Oh, they were beastly and sly, like—like monkeys or—or goats! She should never, never have made it up with Dolly Harris! She would never speak to her again!

She stood up and stalked around the curtain toward the door. Yes! She was right! There they were—the pair of them—laughing like cats! It was horrible—worse than she'd supposed. Dolly actually had her hand on that odious Mr. Top-Morlion's shoulder as if she'd just been whispering in his ear!

"Oh, *Maggie*!" cried Dolly, killing herself with laughter.

"Oh, *Dolly*!" said Maggie, as if she would gladly have helped. "Get out of my way!"

Before Dorothy could move, Maggie Hemp's anger boiled over and she gave Philip Top-Morlion a sharp push.

At once there was a grating sound, as of a cello being freed from a doorway, and Philip Top-Morlion, with a hoarse cry, flew backwards down the two steps.

Dorothy, still holding on to the straps she'd been trying to unfasten, accompanied him, and, with a painful clashing of noses, they completed their journey in the street outside. As on their previous meeting they lay in each other's arms, mightily surprised.

"Are—are you hurt, Miss Harris?" asked Philip, feeling dazed, his eyes watering.

"Oh, no, no! Are *you* hurt, Mr. Top-Morlion?"

"No, no! Not at all . . ."

"But why don't you ask *me*?" sobbed Maggie Hemp, standing in the doorway and trembling with rage. "Why don't you ask Maggie Hemp if *she's* been hurt? Why don't you, you—you hyenas, you!"

Chapter Eleven

MAGGIE Hemp rushed away from Bartholomews, half blinded with tears. They were all laughing at her! People were even staring out of Collier's big window and laughing! She could *never* go there again! Her whole life was ruined!

Dolly Harris, lying on the dirty ground and showing a good deal more of her stumpy legs than she needed to, was laughing till she cried, and so was that snaky Top-Morlion, all tumbled up beside her!

Oh, tears are cheap, aren't they! But not the boiling, scalding ones that ran down Maggie's cheeks as she ran and ran with her hands to her ears.

All the world was laughing at her, and she couldn't bear the sound of it. It was a horrible world! You only had to look around a curtain, and what did you find? Grins and slyness going on behind your back! Everybody despised you if you were honest.

It was indeed a cruel world for people like Maggie Hemp, who couldn't keep a lover for more than a week because she just couldn't help telling him things for his own good.

Poor, pretty Maggie Hemp whom nobody understood! Surely there was somebody, somewhere, who would see, wide blue eye to wide blue eye, with her.

She stumbled along with her eyes awash and her nose growing as red as a berry. She'd been so happy to have made things up with Dolly Harris, and talked about what they should wear for the night of the comet on Devil's Dyke! Now it was over forever!

The comet! She hated it. She wished that stupid Pigott had never invented it. If she did go to watch it, it would have to be with her dull-as-ditchwater ma and pa, who'd talk about beef and pork and sausages all the time. Never! She'd sit at home and sew rather than that!

She sniffed and sobbed her way through the narrow, twisting Lanes, with hateful images of jeers and sneers and whispers cut off short thronging her brain. She never really noticed, as she passed, that many was the head that turned, and many the sympathetic smile, for the pretty, brokenhearted girl.

"Sure to God they're not tears, me darlin'?" came a voice in her ear, together with a strong smell of spirits in the air. " 'Tis the mornin' dew on yer cheeks—for ye're as pretty as a primrose, and I don't tell a lie!"

It was Cassidy, who'd been loafing outside the King's Head. He was bandaged as if he'd been embalmed, for O'Rourke had told him that Mary Flatley herself was coming down with some liniment, and he wanted to show her he needed it. Though he might have done with a roll or two less of the bandage and not come to any harm, it was, as he said to O'Rourke, but a couple of yards of white lie.

"Oh, please go away!" sobbed Maggie Hemp, mightily embarrassed by the Irishman, who stank of brandy. "Or I'll call for help!"

But there was no getting rid of Cassidy as easily as that. The very sight of a female in tears was more intoxicating to him than all the brandy that ever came out of France . . . there not being a drop of good Irish whiskey to be had in the King's Head for love or money.

And talking of love, who was it who had made her so unhappy? Say but the word and Cassidy would give his right arm! Or was it that she'd lost a lover by drowning, maybe? It was a fate very common among them who lived by the sea!

If that was it, then she should dry her eyes and consider that more good men came out of the sea than ever went into it, and they were like pebbles on the shore.

"So give over weepin', me darlin'," said Cassidy. He held out his green arms and took Maggie Hemp's surprised hand into his own two bandaged ones, holding it as if it had been a rare and delicate butterfly.

So that was how he was standing, like a whited sepulcher, holding a pretty girl's hand and calling her "darlin'," when Mary Flatley, in her best dress and shawl, with a bottle of liniment, a basket of apples, and her last drop of good whiskey, came running down to give him her heart.

She stopped as if she'd been shot, and her eyes blazed up so that Cassidy felt the heat of them, though he was six yards off and trying to look the other way.

"Ye dirty scoundrel!" she cried. "Smarmin' up to another bit of muslin skirt! Me mother was right, Michael Cassidy! Ye've not even the decency to be dead!"

Away she went like whirlwind, and Cassidy, whose bandages were like shackles, was left far behind.

She flew through The Lanes, losing apples from her basket as fast as tears. She was off for the fishmonger's son! She'd marry him now—this very minute! He'd only to say the word. Though he was quiet and a bit on the dull side, at least he was honest and true!

She rushed across Bartholomews toward Saunders', and there, standing next door and smiling to herself, as if all were well with the world, was the doctor's speckle-eyed daughter, the one with the poky little face!

" 'Tis no use yer smilin'!" sobbed Mary Flatley. "For he'll break yer heart as soon as spit! He's found another, so ye've lost him even before ye had him, the dirty, philanderin' rogue!"

Then she vanished inside Saunders' and was lost among huge hanging nets and clusters of green glass floats.

Chapter Twelve

Lost him? thought Dorothy Harris. The girl's out of her mind! She stared into Saunders' and was confronted by the slow grins of several huge fishermen who loomed out of the marine gloom like monsters of the deep.

She retreated and shook her head. If the girl had really meant Philip Top-Morlion, then she'd never made a bigger mistake in her life.

She smiled. Although she was mildly shocked that Philip should have been mixed up with the Irish girl, there was no doubt it gave him a touch of mystery that wasn't at all displeasing.

Anyway, he was coming to give her her lesson at nine o'clock that very evening. He'd have come earlier, but the bridge of his father's cello had been broken when they'd fallen down the steps, and he had to get it repaired.

He'd asked if nine o'clock was too late. No, she'd said, but wasn't it inconvenient for him? Surely he had more exciting things to do with his evenings than to give young ladies lessons on the cello?

"More exciting things than music?" he'd asked seriously.

"I love music," she'd said. "Better than anything."

"So do I," said he.

"Till nine o'clock, then?"

"On the very stroke, Miss Harris."

Well! If that was losing him, then give her more such losses! She would bear them with equanimity. If only she could keep him off Bach, Handel, and Bononcini, she was absolutely certain he'd ask her to go with him to Devil's Dyke on Saturday night.

She went home and set about making herself hauntingly beautiful. This necessitated dressing and undressing some twenty times and waiting for suitable moments to enter her mother's room and borrow articles of jewelry and French scent.

By five o'clock she was ready and faced the prospect of sitting in her room, like a vase, for four hours.

Twelve of them passed, and it was half-past five. She put her ear to her clock. It was still going.

"Dorothy?"

"Yes, Mama?"

"What are you doing?"

"Nothing, Mama."

"You're very quiet."

"Yes, Mama."

"Dorothy?"

"Yes, Mama?"

"Have you been using my scent?"

"No, Mama."

"Then why can I smell it all over the house?"

"I can't smell anything, Mama."

At seven o'clock she was summoned for dinner. She couldn't eat. At half past seven she remembered her cello and began to look for it. At eight o'clock she was still looking. At a quarter past eight she saw her brother leaving the house.

She called down to him from her window. "Have you seen my cello?"

Harris looked up. "Cello?" he said wonderingly.

"Yes. My cello. Have you seen it?"

"When?"

"Now!"

Harris looked around carefully.

"No."

She stared after him thoughtfully, then went back to searching for her vanished instrument. Harris went down to the beach.

Bostock was by the breakwater. He was wearing a blue cape with silver frogs, and an expensive wig that lay on his head like an old salad.

They had been presented to Captain Bostock by Mrs. Bostock on the occasion of his elevation to the Bench, as she wanted him to look like a gentleman.

The friends shook hands.

"Harris?" said Bostock.

"Yes, Bosty?"

"Do you really think that—"

"I don't *think*," said Harris, silencing his friend with a smile. "I *know*. It's science, Bosty, and science means to *know*, not to *think*."

Bostock nodded.

"Harris?"

"Yes, Bosty?"

"Don't you think we ought to be going?"

"In a little while, old friend. In just a little while."

They sat in silence, dreaming their dreams. From time to time Bostock stole a glance at Harris and marveled that a head that was really quite small could contain a brain so large.

Little by little the sky darkened. The stars winked and the friends left the beach with a noise like pearls.

They walked, still in silence, to Harris's house. Lights shone from all the upper windows. Harris pointed.

"That's hers!"

Bostock blushed and stared.

Harris pulled him away and around to the other side of the house.

"What is it, Harris?"

Harris raised his finger to his lips and, with infinite caution, removed his sister's cello from the stone coffin in which he had concealed it.

The learned article on Courtship had stated music, vocal or instrumental, so Harris, anxious to take no chances and to leave no stone unturned, had decided on both.

"Oh, Harris! You think of everything!"

Harris nodded. He did.

"I'll kill him!" gasped Dorothy, aloft.

The time for her lesson drawing near, she had been watching from her window when she'd seen her hateful brother stealthily lifting her lost cello from its hiding place.

"I'll kill him! *And* that idiot friend of his!"

She rushed from her window and returned with a bowl of dirty water. Then, hearing the unmistakable grumble of a cello below, flung out the water with an enraged screech.

"Take that, you filthy little beast!"

She missed them. Harris and Bostock, capering deftly, arrived back under Mary's window, panting and unscathed. They did not even suspect the narrowness of their escape.

They looked up. Mary's window was open to the spring night. Harris twanged the cello and, marvel of marvels, Mary appeared! Harris felt quite awed by his own success. It was happening exactly as he'd seen it happen that morning, through the telescope. The girl had been drawn to her window by an instinct she could not deny. What had moved one Mary was quite definitely moving another.

She looked down. She saw Bostock and Harris. She made a noise like a rocket and vanished from view.

"In Dublin's fair city," croaked Bostock, while Harris twanged loudly by his side.

"Where girls are so pretty . . ."

Mary came back.

"I first set my eyes on sweet Molly Malone!"

Mary beckoned. Bostock approached, and Mary emptied the contents of a chamber pot over Captain Bostock's cloak and wig.

It was five minutes after nine o'clock and the last echoes of Bostock's cry of anguish had died away. Dorothy Harris waited by her window, listening for the sound of her admirer's step.

At ten o'clock she began to cry. At eleven o'clock she was still crying. At twelve o'clock she blew out her candle, got undressed, and went to bed.

The Irish girl had been right all the time. He *had* found someone else. Philip Top-Morlion had not come.

She cried herself to sleep, sobbing, over and over again, "Why, why didn't you come?"

In point of fact he had come. And on the very stroke of nine. He'd glimpsed her at her window and had had the happy idea of announcing his presence, not by a commonplace knock on the door, but with a melodious flourish from his grand symphony, on his father's cello. What could have been more romantic than that?

He had been rewarded with a stream of filthy water and a loud screech of abuse. He had fled, soaked to the skin. He had never been so insulted in all his life!

Chapter Thirteen

Next morning Philip Top-Morlion rose from his bed, shuffled across his room, and, blinking in the sunlight, put his hand out of the window. Sure enough, there was his coat and shirt, where they'd been hanging out to dry, like a suicide.

He shuddered. It was all true. It had actually happened to him. It hadn't been a horrible dream. She really had thrown water all over him.

Why—why? What had he done to offend her? He was used to being ignored, he was used to being slighted, but he was not used to being soaked to the skin and called a filthy little beast!

It was the end. He hated the world. He wanted to die on her doorstep with, if possible, an explanatory note attached: "This is your doing. I hope you are satisfied."

And he might die, too. Sensitive people like him caught chills very easily. You were always reading about them, coughing their lungs up in a garret and being found by their landlady, dead and with a flower of blood coming out of their mouths.

Already he was beginning to feel feverish. He dressed and ate a hurried breakfast. He ought to see a doctor. It was foolish to neglect himself.

Unfortunately, the nearest physician was Dr. Harris —*her* father. Well, it couldn't be helped. His health came first. If it meant swallowing his pride before he swallowed any medicine, then he'd do it. Posterity would never have forgiven him if he'd sacrificed himself so young.

He put on his cello, took up his flute, fiddle, and music case, and walked unsteadily to *her* street and stood outside *her* house. He wondered if, by any chance, she could see him. He crossed to the other side of the street to give her a better chance. He coughed three or four times and looked exceptionally frail.

He couldn't see her, and he felt very angry indeed. He crossed back again. Perhaps she'd be in the hall when he asked the maid if he could see the doctor. He'd ignore her. Or, better, he'd give one deep, accusing look that would strike her to the heart. That is, if she had a heart.

He knocked on the door. The maid answered.

"I'll go and tell Miss Harris you're here," she said, and went before he could even open his mouth to say that she was the last person he wanted to see.

He was about to go away when there was Miss Harris, coming down the stairs, two at a time, in a blossomy gown and looking like a storm in an orchard. She looked flushed and eager. He wondered if she'd dare to beg his pardon?

Dorothy Harris, who had been watching Philip Top-Morlion from behind her curtain, wondered if *he* had come to beg *her* pardon.

She couldn't understand why else he should have been loitering on the other side of the street like a criminal and clearing his throat. Perhaps he really had come to explain that something extraordinary had happened last night that had prevented his keeping the appointment?

And would she forgive him, after all she'd suffered? Of course she would! Only—only she'd be dignified about it. She wouldn't just throw herself at his head. She'd had quite enough of that! She'd be a little cool and distant to begin with. She'd show him that she had her pride.

"Well?" she asked breathlessly. "What is it that you want, Mr. Top-Morlion?"

Can't she see how ill I look? thought Philip. Can't she see that I need a doctor?

"I—I would like to see your father, Miss Harris."

"My father? Why?"

"I think you can guess, Miss Harris," he said quietly.

He wants to *marry* me! thought Dorothy with a rush of amazement. He wants to ask Pa for my hand! Oh, no! He can't—he mustn't! It—it's ridiculous! Oh, I like him well enough . . . but I hardly know him! Besides, I'm much too young to think about getting married! Perhaps he doesn't know I'll only be sixteen in July. I know I look older, but—but—Oh, dear! This is awful!

"I—I think you ought to wait a little while, Mr. Top-Morlion," she said with a nervous smile.

"How long?" asked Philip.

"About a—a year?"

My God! thought Philip incredulously. A year to see the doctor? And in my state of health? She really hasn't got a heart at all!

"Thank you!" he said bitterly. "Thank you very much. But, under the circumstances, I think I'd better find someone else."

He tottered away, coughing consumptively.

Dorothy stared after him, unable to believe her ears. So! Just like that! *I think I'd better find someone else.*

It was horrible! Women were *nothing* to a man like that! The Irish girl had been right all along! He really would break your heart as soon as spit!

She ran back up to her room and slammed the door with a violence that shook the house. She sat on her bed, breathing tempestuously and not knowing whether to scream or cry.

What evil fate was forever crossing her path so that, whenever she offered her heart, it was thrown back in her face? What had she done to deserve it?

She began to sob. Perhaps in a year or two she'd have taken such things in her stride, even as, a year or two before, she wouldn't have been walking that way at all. But now she was in the middle of it. Every shadow was a pit and the very morning sunshine was a gilded iron cage.

Presently she grew a little calmer. A man like that wasn't worth crying over. She sniffed and, remembering that it was only Friday, wondered if there was any chance at all of making things up with Maggie Hemp before Saturday night. She felt dreadful about it, but what else could she do?

She stood up and looked in her glass. Maggie would be bound to notice she'd been crying. Oh, well, maybe it was for the best! Maggie might feel sorry for her and be kind.

She changed her April dress for one that had a touch of March about it and suggested blossoms blasted in the bud, and left the house. She walked quickly until she came to the row of smart new villas at the top of the street.

"And have ye taken pity on him, me darlin'?" inquired Cassidy, stepping out from where he'd been loafing at the side door of the house where Mary Flatley worked. "For ye'll never forgive yerself if he dies of a broken heart!"

She stared at him with hatred. She'd like to have known just when and where Philip Top-Morlion was going to die as she would like to have watched.

The side door opened and someone came out. Dorothy hurried away, as she didn't want to be caught in conversation with the shabby Irishman. Anyway, people didn't die of broken hearts! *Her* heart was broken and she'd never felt better in her life!

She reached Collier's and there was Maggie Hemp sitting in the window just like old times! Dear Maggie! She went in.

"You look terrible, Dolly," said Maggie with affectionate satisfaction. "Like something the cat's brought in."

Dorothy sat down.

"Oh, Maggie!" Then, "I—I was wondering if you think I ought to wear my blue velvet cape for Saturday night?" asked Dorothy.

Miss Hemp compressed her lips. She knew perfectly well that something had gone wrong with Dolly's plans and she was trying to make things up as if nothing had happened.

But she wasn't going to let her. She wanted Dolly to be honest with her. If they were going to be friends again, then there were going to be no secrets or slyness.

"You've been crying," she said.

"Are—are you going to wear your lovely new silver dress, Maggie?"

"Your eyes are all red and puffy, Dolly, like giblets."

"I—thought of wearing my grey one . . . if you think it would look all right, Maggie?"

"I do believe you're *still* crying, Dolly!"

"I'm not!"

"Yes, you are! All over your cake. Look!"

"Oh, Maggie!"

"Tell me about it, Dolly. Tell me everything. After all, we *are* friends!"

She had moved closer, to comfort her unhappy friend and to screen her from curious eyes, when she became aware that she was being watched through the window.

Of all people, it was the drunken Irishman who'd accosted her yesterday in The Lanes. She remembered he'd called her "darlin'" and held her hand.

She shook a warning finger. He responded by raising his own in salute.

Dorothy looked up, and Cassidy saluted again.

"Do you know him, dear?"

"No! No!" said Dorothy quickly. "I don't know him from Adam! Do *you* know him?"

"Of course not, dear."

"I wonder why he waved?"

"Oh, you know what men are, dear!"

Dorothy nodded. She knew. They were beasts, they were brutes, and they would break your heart as soon as spit!

Maggie smiled tenderly. She was glad they were of one mind. They were friends again. She held Dorothy's hand and together they sat, in Collier's window, two frail females alone in a forest of monkeys, weasels, vipers and—and MEN. But nothing would come between them any more. Nothing would separate them again.

She gestured angrily through the glass, and Cassidy went away.

Chapter Fourteen

CASSIDY, having applied at the villa, had been told that it was Mary Flatley's day off and that she wouldn't be back till late.

"And where might she be spendin' it, ma'am?"

"With Andrews, of course. The fishmonger's son."

"No!" said Cassidy, white as a ghost.

"Yes!" said the housekeeper. "And a lucky girl she is!"

"Don't tell me they're courtin', ma'am?"

"I'll tell you what I like, young man!"

"And him an Englishman?"

"Every decent, hard-working inch! He's Mr. Saunders' sister's boy. Mr. Saunders, with the shop in Bartholomews."

"The villain!" Cassidy had cried. "The dirty philanderin' villain!" And away he'd gone to Bartholomews, hoping to plead with Mary Flatley before it was too late.

He saluted the two young ladies in Collier's window

and then went inside Saunders' Marine Stores and Fishing Tackle, where he blundered about among rods, lines, hooks, choppers, yellow boots, and terrible festooning nets, like a frantic green fish with a bandaged head.

At length, finding no one about, he stopped and scratched his head.

"In Dublin's fair city," he began to sing, in a small voice as if he'd swallowed a tiny Irishman, "where girls are so pretty . . ."

He peered into the ill-lit depths of the shop, hoping that his song would draw the girl out. Instead, it drew the proprietor, a hard, knobbly man with a nose like a shrimp.

"Yes?"

"I was wonderin', sir, if ye're acquainted with a lass by the name o' Mary Flatley? She's black hair and—"

"I am."

"And have ye seen her this mornin', sir?"

"I have."

"And where might she be, sir?"

"Out with my sister's boy."

"And where might they be walkin', sir . . . if it's not too much trouble to ask?"

"They ain't walking. Wears out boots. They're in the boat."

"At sea?"

"Well, they ain't rowing down North Street!"

Cassidy hurried from the shop and went down to the beach. He stared wildly over the water, but the sun, spilling all over it, turned it to a sea of fire and blinded him.

The only vessel he could see was in his mind's eye, and it was a grand painted barge with a tasseled canopy, under which sat Mary Flatley and Andrews, side by side.

Cassidy groaned as he thought of Andrews, with his crafty silver tongue, offering Mary Flatley the kingdom of the sea, with cockles big enough to ride in, and mackerels, proud as bishops, to draw her along.

"But what of me Michael Cassidy, who's followed me so far and loved me so long?" said she with a wistful smile.

"Forget that no-good Irish loafer! What can he do for you that an Englishman can't do ten times better?"

"Ye dirty lyin' rogue!" wailed Cassidy, stamping and stumbling along the beach and not looking where he was going, for it didn't matter any more.

"Will you wed me, Mary Flatley?" asked Andrews, smooth as silk. "And become a decent English-woman?"

"That I will!" said she with a sigh. "If ye happen to have such a thing as a ring?"

"A ring?" said he with a laugh, and straightway produced an article with a pearl the size of an egg, maybe.

"Don't take it! I'll give ye a diamond as big as an apple!" cried Cassidy, though he'd no more than a shilling and the life he stood up in.

He stumbled on till he came to a breakwater half sunk in the sea, so that its last posts poked up out of the water like a row of executed heads.

He climbed over it, still looking out to sea, and came down on the other side and trod on something soft.

It was a coat and a pair of breeches, huddled in a

heap. Beside them lay a pair of battered boots and stockings, wrinkled like empty worms.

"You're standing on somebody's property," came a cold voice from the shadow of the breakwater.

Cassidy started and then saw it was the pale and brainy boy to whom he'd taken the telescope. He was sitting against the breakwater, shrouded in darkness, with the instrument firmly to his eye.

Cassidy begged his pardon for any inconvenience and hoisted himself back onto the breakwater and continued to scour the sea.

At last he saw the boat. It was not so far out as he'd been looking, nor so grand as he'd feared. It lay no more than sixty yards away, to the west of a line of nets with green glass floats winking and sparkling like emeralds of the deep.

It was a rowboat with shipped oars that stuck up like ears, and the sea kept shrugging it in and out of a pool of sunshine so that it came and went like a dream.

At one end sat Mary Flatley, as small as a thimble, and at the other sat Andrews, as big as a house. Cassidy shuddered at the size of him. A man like that could have given a girl a hundred pound and not even missed it!

Even as Cassidy watched, the big fellow fumbled in his pocket and then held out his hand. Was he giving her a ring?

"What's he doin' out there?" groaned Cassidy.

"None of your business," said Harris from the shadows below.

"Maybe not," said Cassidy sadly. "But what's he givin' her? Can ye tell me that, young sir?"

"Yes," said Harris, not taking his eye from the telescope. "It's what you might call an inedible but otherwise stimulating object. It's part of the ritual of Courtship, you know."

"And is she takin' it?" asked Cassidy, his worst fears confirmed.

"It'll knock her flat," said Harris confidently.

"Oh, Mary, Mary! How could ye?"

"Instinct," said Harris. "She can't help herself."

"Will ye lend me a squint through the glass, young sir, so's I can see for meself?"

"No," said Harris.

"I'll give ye a shillin', young sir."

"No."

"Ye're a hard case!" said Cassidy bitterly. "An Englishman through and through."

He began to make his way to the end of the breakwater so he could see for himself what was going on in the boat, while the hard case remained in possession of the telescope below.

Now Harris was not a hard case. In fact he considered himself to be quite warmhearted. He'd not parted with the telescope because of Bostock. He did not want Bostock's present activities to be witnessed by eyes other than his own.

Bostock, as Harris had inferred, was engaged in procuring the inedible but otherwise stimulating object mentioned in the learned article on Courtship, the presentation of which was destined to knock Mary flat. Mary Harris, not Mary Flatley—for what the devil did she have to do with it anyway?

Music, both vocal and instrumental, having met with a conspicuous lack of success, Bostock had naturally been depressed. In fact, he'd turned quite nasty, and Harris had had quite a struggle with him.

Patiently Harris had pointed out that failures, however disagreeable, were really a good thing. It stood to reason. The more you failed, the less chance there was of failing next time. You were reducing the chance of error by using it up. That was science. Did Bostock not know that nothing great had ever been achieved without many mistakes on the way? How many baths did Bostock think Archimedes had to take before the water overflowed?

Bostock had pointed out that there'd been an overflow from Mary's window the first time, and that was enough for him. But Harris, explaining the easy success in courtship of foolish creatures like herons, magpies, and oyster catchers, at last persuaded Bostock that the presentation of prey or of inedible but otherwise stimulating objects was worth a try.

The particular objects to which Harris had directed Bostock's attention were the green glass floats used by fishermen to hold up their nets. Mary already had three of them, hanging over her bed like a pawnshop, and Harris assured Bostock that another pair would send her wild with delight.

Bostock said he didn't have any money, as he'd given Harris his last fourpence ha'penny. Harris said not to worry, as Bostock could nick them from the nets floating out at sea.

It was quite all right, Harris explained, because as long as they were floating, they were flotsam, and, as such, belonged to the Crown. But, as it wasn't to be supposed that the king wanted them, he, Bostock, had the law on his side—which any court in the land would uphold.

All that was needed was a strong swimmer and a sharp knife, to cut the floats free from the nets.

Bostock was the swimmer, and the knife was a handsome, ivory-handled article that had been presented to Captain Bostock by the Brighton Exploring Society on the occasion of his election to the presidency, and was engraved with his name. It had been the sharpest knife Bostock had been able to find.

So now Harris waited confidently in the shadow for the triumphant return of his friend, while not very far away Cassidy squatted forlornly on the last stump of the breakwater like a green frog with brass buttons that had missed its chance of being kissed into a prince.

He stared at the rowboat as hard as he could. What was going on out there? What was he saying to her, and she to him? What had he given her? Had he really parted with a ring? What was a ring to a big Englishman like that?

The Englishman had not parted with a ring. In fact he hadn't parted with anything more than a lump of stale bread he'd given to Mary Flatley to feed the seagulls with.

Andrews was a huge, good-natured youth, the color of a kipper, and as straight and true as a plank of wood, but he was a bit on the stingy side.

Mary Flatley was his second girl, the first having

given up after he'd spent no more than a shilling on her in eighteen months, and then when it was raining.

He was, you might have said, a careful youth who was saving up for something, but he never said what, as he was a bit close with words, too.

"Are ye savin' up for a house, maybe?" said Mary Flatley, scattering all the crumbs at once. "Or a fine new boat of yer own to bring home fish for yer wife and little ones when ye have 'em?"

Andrews, of the silver tongue, looked down at his knees and smiled at them affably.

"A penny for yer thoughts, Mr. Andrews!" said Mary Flatley.

He looked up with interest.

"Eh?"

Mary Flatley sighed and reflected that, if it hadn't been for that smarmy, faithless Cassidy, she'd not have been sitting here now, as flat as a drink of water. She hated him; she loved him. He was her worst friend and her best enemy.

"I was thinkin'," said Andrews, as if still pursuing the offered penny, "that we might row over to the nets and look at the fish. That's what I was thinking."

"If ye're sure they'll not charge us for it?" said Mary Flatley.

"No," said Andrews. "It's all the same to them."

"Then let's take a look," said Mary Flatley. "For it's all the same to me, too." .

He spat on his hands, and, grasping the oars, began to row vigorously toward the nets. Mary Flatley, sitting in the stern, watched the blades rising and falling like choppers. She gazed over them to the beach. Sitting on the end of the dwindling breakwater was a lump of green that looked a bit like Cassidy.

She waved. The lump waved back. She stood up and waved again. The boat rocked and Andrews clouted the water with a steadying blade.

At once there was a scream and a terrible bubbling howl! Something wild and streaming, with a knife between its teeth, came up on the end of the oar. It was Bostock.

"Harris!" shrieked Bostock, who, having been struck on the head, was seeing a great many stars, suns, moons, and comets without the aid of any telescope whatsoever. "HARRIS!"

Captain Bostock's ivory-handled knife fell out of Bostock's mouth and vanished into the sea, where it sank and, doubtless, became jetsam and the property of the Crown.

Bostock shrieked again. Mary Flatley screamed and Andrews struggled to dislodge the monster from his oar. Knowing nothing of Bostock, his hopes, his dreams, his abiding love for Mary Harris, nor the learned article on Courtship that was responsible for his appearance, the occupants of the little boat could only regard him with terror and revulsion and fight to escape his grasp.

Bostock, still dazed from the blow, fought back and overturned the boat.

Now Cassidy entered the lists. He stripped off his coat, plunged into the sea, and sank like a stone. He couldn't swim a stroke, but he'd seen his girl in danger of drowning, and he meant to save her even if it killed the pair of them.

He came up roaring water and waving his arms; then he went down again to the bottom of the sea. His past life flashed before his eyes and he didn't regret a minute of it, though he wished it had been longer and a bit more drawn out.

He came up five times in all, for you can't drown an Irishman in three; then Andrews got hold of him by the hair and dragged him up onto the beach.

He'd seen Cassidy in difficulties, and, leaving Mary Flatley safely holding on to the boat, he'd swum to his rival's aid. He was truly a good-natured youth, as kind and brave as any knight, so long as there wasn't any expense.

Back went Andrews for the boat, and, with himself and Mary Flatley astride the keel, paddled away for shore.

"He's dead!" cried Mary Flatley, rushing to the sodden Cassidy, from whom water was running like whiskey on St. Patrick's night.

Andrews picked him up and held him upside down till the rest of the water came out. Then he laid him down, and Cassidy opened his eyes.

"He's alive!" cried Mary Flatley. "Mr. Andrews, ye've saved Michael Cassidy's life!"

Andrews stared down at his feet, affably.

"Oh, Cassidy!" cried Mary Flatley, kneeling down beside him and wringing the sea out of his hair. "Did ye hear that? Mr. Andrews has saved yer life! So what can I do, me darlin', but wed him today, if he asks? For I've nothin' else to give him for his trouble but me hand and me heart!"

"Oh, Mary, Mary!" groaned Cassidy. "I'd never have needed savin' at all if it hadn't been for the love I bear yerself! I'd nothin' else to give ye but me life!"

"But ye're still alive, Michael Cassidy, so what's the use of that?"

Chapter Fifteen

THE beach was empty. The unlucky boating party and the passers-by who'd stopped to watch had all departed. Nothing remained but a large wet patch on the stones, compounded of seawater and tears. The scene was finished. It was time for the others to take their bow.

Bostock and Harris emerged from the shadow of the breakwater. Bostock, due to the action of the sea, was looking peculiarly clean, like a scraped potato. Harris was supporting him, as he was still weak from his exertions and unable to speak.

They went first to Harris's house. Harris concealed the telescope in the stone coffin while Bostock looked on with chattering teeth.

Then they went to Bostock's. Harris observed that the Irishmen's cart was once more outside, but there was no sign of the owners.

They went into the house through the side door and Harris helped Bostock upstairs.

There was a long, lugubrious face at the window. It was O'Rourke. He had replaced the broken pane and was engaged in cleaning his own finger and nose marks from the new glass.

He took no notice of the two boys. Unlike his partner, he did not feel talkative when he was high up. He was terrified of heights.

Bostock began to take down the ships' posters with Mary Harris's name on them.

"What are you doing that for, Bosty?"

"It's finished, Harris. It's all over."

He rolled up the posters, tied them with a piece of string, and laid them on his bed. Idly Harris picked up a roll and, applying it to his eye, observed Bostock.

"It's still only Friday, Bosty. There's still time—"

"It's no good! Everything's ruined now!"

"Oh, Bosty, how little you understand!" said Harris. "We've only just started! We've only just scratched the surface of things! That's why they look such a mess! Nothing's ruined, old friend!"

He explained that there was still a great deal more in the learned article on Courtship that they hadn't tried. It would be madness to give up now. For instance, there was—

Bostock lost his temper. When he'd said everything was ruined, he hadn't been talking about the learned article. He had been referring to his pa's best coat, his best hat, his best wig and cape, and, most recently of all, the knife that had been presented to him by the Brighton Exploring Society and had been engraved with his name. His pa had been very proud of that knife and used it to peel apples when company came. Gone!

In view of all this, didn't Harris think that he, Bostock, had sacrificed enough?

Harris, somewhat taken aback by Bostock's outburst, remarked that Mark Antony had sacrificed a whole empire for Cleopatra, so wasn't Bostock being a little close-fisted about Mary? And anyway, Captain Bostock was a sick man and not in any state to discover his losses before Christmas.

He turned the rolled-up posters toward the window and peered past O'Rourke into the distance, as if to demonstrate how far away Christmas was.

But Bostock, who always looked forward to Christmas as a time of warmth and presents and kindness from his parents, was enraged by the thought of having even that snatched from his grasp. He glared at Harris, and, being reminded by the roll of posters of yet another item in the catalogue of his father's missing property, said, "And I want the telescope back!"

Harris stiffened. He removed the roll from his eye and stared at it as if it were the ghost of the fine brass instrument that was so close to his heart. He stood up.

"I'm going now, Bosty."

"The telescope, Harris!"

"Good-bye, Bosty."

"Harris!"

But Harris had gone, and without shaking hands. Bostock stared at the closed door, at first with anger, then with bewilderment and dismay.

At first he wanted to run after Harris and tell him

he hadn't meant what he'd said, but he was still too deeply hurt by Harris's abrupt departure. He wondered if he ought to wait for Harris to come back and then tell him it was all right.

"Oh, Harris!" he whispered. "Even if I never get Mary, you can keep the telescope!"

The door opened. It wasn't Harris. It was the housekeeper. She looked around the room and frowned at Bostock.

"You're for it!" she said.

Bostock smiled feebly. She always said that.

"Where have you put it?"

"Put what?"

She shook a polishing rag menacingly. "You know what I mean."

Bostock knew. She meant the brass telescope.

Ordinarily it was not an article that interested the good lady, but, having seen the recent commotion at sea from an upstairs window, she'd gone to polish the master's telescope and look through it, in case anybody she knew was drowning.

It hadn't been there, so her thoughts had gone to Bostock.

"If it's not back today, I'll tell the master," she said. "And then you'll be for it!"

Her tone of voice suggested that, if Bostock did not comply with her demand, he could count himself lucky that the house wasn't equipped with a yardarm, as he'd undoubtedly be hanged from it.

"But—but I haven't got it!" he moaned. "Whatever it is! Word of honor!"

He didn't know what to do. He thought with anguish of what would happen if he asked Harris for the telescope again, and he thought with equal anguish of what would happen if he didn't. There seemed no way out.

The housekeeper, unmoved, repeated her threat, and then, raising her eyes, saw O'Rourke's absorbed face at the window.

The thought crossed her mind that, in spite of appearances and everything she knew about him, Master Bostock might be innocent, and those no-good Irish loafers might be to blame.

She glared at O'Rourke and remembered his partner, who, she suspected, was as crooked as his nose. So she said, as loudly as she could, "I'll give you till tonight to put it back. Either that or I'll go straight to your father, Captain Bostock, *J.P.*!"

She had the satisfaction of seeing Bostock on the point of collapse, and O'Rourke in a similar state as he vanished below the sill.

Chapter Sixteen

Y<small>E</small> dirty thief, Cassidy!"
shouted O'Rourke, coming violently into their little
room in the King's Head, where Cassidy was sitting
before the empty grate, wrapped in a blanket, with his
wet shirt hanging out the window and his dripping
breeches depending from the mantelpiece, for he was
a modest man.

"Say that again, O'Rourke," cried Cassidy, rising
like the ghost of Julius Caesar—the blanket being full
of holes, "and I'll knock ye down!"

"Then I'll not make a murderer of ye as well," said
O'Rourke. "So I'll keep me opinions to meself till ye're
hanged for 'em!"

But he couldn't. He was too angry and frightened.
He began pulling out Cassidy's belongings, going
through his pockets and looking under the bed, raging
and railing at Cassidy all the time.

"What are ye lookin' for?" demanded Cassidy,

being pushed from wall to bed and back again as he got in the way of the search.

What was O'Rourke looking for? Well might Cassidy ask! He was looking for whatever it was that Cassidy had thieved out of the magistrate's house.

O'Rourke, having heard the housekeeper's threat, jumped at once to the conclusion that Cassidy had been guilty of backsliding. It was as plain as the nose on Cassidy's face. He'd lost Mary Flatley, so he cared nothing for anybody any more. The loss of the love that had turned him into an angel had put him right back among the devils again.

O'Rourke was almost in tears. Hadn't he watched over Cassidy like a father and humored him every yard of the way? And now Cassidy repaid him by stealing out of the house of the very gentleman who could have them both hanged!

In vain Cassidy protested that he was as innocent as a newborn babe. O'Rourke was too mad to listen; he'd been frightened to death by the housekeeper and the gallows glare in her eyes.

Then Cassidy, who'd been racking his brains for the cause of it all, remembered the brass telescope. O'-Rourke collapsed on the bed.

"Then ye *did* steal it?"

"Never! I gave it straight into the hand of the doctor's son. I swear it, O'Rourke!"

"Did he give ye money for it?"

"Fourpence ha'penny for me trouble."

"Then it's trouble indeed, Cassidy! Ye're worse than a thief. Ye're a receiver of stolen property, and as such ye're liable to the full strength of the law!"

"Never!"

O'Rourke looked at him pityingly, then went to his carpetbag and took out a battered book. It was a volume entitled *The English Lawyer*. O'Rourke had stolen it from a bookshop in Liverpool, for how could he keep Cassidy from breaking the laws of the land unless he'd a list of them to know what was what?

He found the page, and Cassidy, following O'-Rourke's huge finger, saw for himself that his friend was quite right. It was all written down, and it proved him to be as guilty as the thief.

He'd get fourteen years' transportation if he was lucky. Otherwise he'd be hanged. And poor O'-Rourke, being party to the criminal, would get the same.

O'Rourke began packing up. They'd have to leave the town at once. Cassidy lay on the bed with the blanket over his head and swore that he'd sooner be hanged than leave Mary Flatley to marry the Englishman. So long as she wasn't a wife, there was still hope, even if it was only to be Cassidy's widow.

O'Rourke dropped Cassidy's bag with a thump.

"Then it's good-bye to ye, Michael Cassidy. I'll not be hanged for another man's girl."

Up came Cassidy's head. "Then ye'll leave me?"

"What good would we be to each other, hangin' on the end of a rope?"

"Could we not get the article put back, O'Rourke?"

"D'ye mean steal it out of the doctor's house?"

"I'm still an honest man, O'Rourke."

"Thank God—else ye'd be hanged twice over!"

"I was thinkin' of goin' to the boy himself. Give me

a chance, O'Rourke! He's only a boy. He's flesh and blood. He's not a boy of stone that would see a man hanged for a bit of brass!"

O'Rourke came back from the door.

"He's flesh and blood, Cassidy," he said, remembering the night in the churchyard. "I'll grant ye that."

"And will ye grant me the chance to try him?"

O'Rourke fumbled in his pocket. He produced a grubby scrap of paper, which was the firm's work-sheet. He consulted it.

"Ye're in luck, Cassidy. There's a window needs mendin' in the doctor's house. It's the window of the boy's own room."

Cassidy leaped from his bed as if it were on fire. He dragged on his breeches and shirt. O'Rourke stood back.

"I'm not saying ye'll fail, Cassidy," he said. "But if ye should and the boy denies ye, will ye promise to come with me out of the town tonight?"

Cassidy promised. How could the boy deny him? Had it been an old man, now, stern and calloused with years and well past the age of loving, it would have been another matter. But a boy, still young and tender enough to cry over a lost kitten, maybe? Ah, there was nothing to it!

They went out together, and even O'Rourke felt that it would have been an unusual boy indeed who could have remained cold and unmoved in the face of Cassidy's love and Cassidy's desperate plight.

The ladder was off the cart and up against the wall almost before the pony had stopped, and Cassidy was halfway up when O'Rourke shouted out, "Ye've forgot the glass!"

But Cassidy went on like a green shoot rising, and, when he came to the broken window, he looked down and waved to O'Rourke. The boy was inside.

Cassidy began to talk through the hole in the glass, and when Cassidy talked, the world stood still. Ah, that Cassidy! He could have charmed the birds from the trees and every lass from her glass! Oh, Cassidy! Who could turn aside from the pleading look on your face? Who could deny you, with your golden tongue? What heart in all the world would not be melted by the aching love of Cassidy for Mary Flatley?

But he was a devil of a long time about it!

Cassidy came down like the weather.

"O'Rourke," he said, "ye'll not believe it, but he *is* a boy of stone. Somebody ought to tell his father, the doctor, and maybe he'll put him in a bottle."

"What did ye say to him, Cassidy?"

"I told him of Mary and me."

"And what did he say to that?"

"Nothin'. He just stared at me with them terrible eyes of his."

"And then what did ye say to him?"

"I told him we'd be a pair of dead men if the instrument wasn't put back in the magistrate's house within the hour."

"And what did he say to that?"

"Nothin'. So I asked him if he'd have us on his conscience just for a bit of brass?"

"And what did he say to *that*?"

"Nothin'."

"And what did ye say to him then?"

"Why, I told him he was made of stone and that if ever I was to meet with him on a dark night, I'd punch him into the middle of next week or further. Let's go, O'Rourke, before I damn meself forever by goin' back and committin' murder on a child!"

They put the ladder on the cart.

"A child!" repeated Cassidy, still unable to take it in. "Now had it been an old man, all crabbed and horny, I could have understood it better. A man like that wouldn't have cared any more for lovers and their sighs. But a child—"

"An old man would have been better, Cassidy," said O'Rourke, jerking the pony into life. "Though he'd have been past love, he'd have remembered it, for it's not somethin' ye're likely to forget. But a child, not yet come to it, can't remember where he's never been!"

"Ye're a charitable man, O'Rourke. Will ye be charitable enough to let me say good-bye to Mary Flatley?"

"That would be foolishness, Cassidy, not charity. It would be cruel to the pair of ye. Let her wed her Englishman in peace, while you and me go lookin' for work."

And he reminded Cassidy that they'd scarcely a shilling left to bless themselves with, being out of pocket to the tune of two pieces of window glass and a third that had been put in at the magistrate's house and not claimed for, on account of O'Rourke's having left in a fright.

They turned the corner at the top of the street.

Cassidy gazed up at the villa where Mary Flatley worked and saw her best green dress hanging out of her window to dry.

"God bless you," he said, "and send you a good life."

He turned to stare back at the house they'd left, and muttered, "And may God forgive ye, if He's a mind to, by keepin' ye out of me way!"

The cart rolled on and took the road to Patcham, and Harris put down the telescope with a deep sigh of relief.

Chapter Seventeen

HARRIS breathed heavily. He was not made of stone. He rejected the Irishman's accusation indignantly. He was human. He was composed of flesh and blood, disposed in vessels and layers about his bones in accordance with the strictest principles of Anatomy. And he was proud of it.

Harris had a liver, a spleen, a sweetbread, and lights, just like anybody else. He also had a heart that drove his blood from place to place and nourished his brain.

It was Harris's brain that was unusual. It was very powerful and helped him to see things more clearly than most people.

He saw, for instance, that the Irishman was a very dangerous and unpleasant fellow and it was a good thing that he'd gone. He saw that he'd been talking through his hat, and that if anybody was going to be hanged for Captain Bostock's telescope it would probably be Bosty, which was unlikely in the extreme.

He wondered if Bostock had put the Irishman up to

it in order to exert pressure on Harris. If so, it would have been blackmail and very wrong. Harris wouldn't countenance anything like that. He was surprised at Bosty.

In short, he was not going to give the telescope back. What would become of Pigott's comet if he did?

Suddenly Pigott's comet became very important and Harris felt that, if he didn't observe it at the proper time, somehow it would be disappointed—as if it were a visitor who'd come a long way to see Harris and found him to be out.

It was quite impossible to give the telescope back. He looked through it again—not at the sky, but at the villa at the top of the street where the green dress was hanging out of the top window. It jumped toward him, almost close enough to touch.

He thought, inexplicably, of Cassidy going up his ladder, and the look on Mary Flatley's face as she'd come in answer to the song. He thought of the night in the churchyard, and O'Rourke's gentle words, and he felt a curious aching sensation in the lower part of his chest.

He shut up the telescope with a snap. It was out of the question to give it back.

He really couldn't. It would be as good—or, rather, as bad—as admitting failure to Bosty. He'd never failed before, and he wasn't going to be pushed into it now, not for a hundred Irishmen and their girls!

He gazed down at the shortened brass cylinder in his hands.

"Keep me!" it seemed to say. "I bring things nearer, almost close enough to touch!"

Harris extended it.

"Almos-ss-st!" hissed the polished joints.

He shut it, and the aching sensation in his chest seemed to spread upward till he felt it in his very teeth. With shaking hands he put the leather caps back on the two glass eyes and blinded them. He left his room, taking the telescope with him. He was very angry.

He went out of the house, slammed the door, and set off down the street. He met Bostock at the corner.

"Harris!" said Bostock with a desperately frightened look. "Have you got the telescope?"

Silently Harris gave it to him. As the instrument left his hands, he had the queerest feeling that he was still looking through it, only through the wrong end. Everything was unutterably remote.

"Oh, Harris! You're a brick!"

"No," said Harris bitterly. "Stone."

He walked away, trembling with a sense of outrage and injustice. He had intended to surprise Bostock with his magnanimity. He'd thought of bursting in upon him when Bosty had given up hope. He'd pictured it all very clearly and had been actually looking forward to it. But now, to have been met on the way, as if Bostock had expected it all the time, was intolerable!

He returned to his house in a state of profound agitation. He'd been treated monstrously. He'd worked hard for Bosty, and now, just when the fruits of victory were within his grasp, they'd been cruelly snatched away.

But Bosty wasn't going to have it both ways! He,

Harris, would see to that! It had always been the tele-scope or Mary. Well, he'd gotten the telescope back, so that was the end of Mary. Once and for all Bostock would see that it was madness to cross Harris. Harris could undo just as well as he could do. Nothing was beyond him.

He went straight to Mary's room. She was sitting on her bed, frizzling up the hair of that little cow Caro-line.

"Go away!" said Caroline. "This is a ladies' room. No boys allowed!"

Harris ignored her and addressed himself to Mary. "Bosty's found somebody else," he said. "Another girl. So he won't be going with you tomorrow night. It's all over."

He made a gesture of wiping his hands of the whole affair and withdrew before he could be questioned further.

That had fixed Bosty! A period had been put to his romantic aspirations, a very full stop indeed. Harris nodded grimly. What he, Harris, put asunder, no man on earth could join together again.

He went to his sister Dorothy's room. She was trim-ming a hat and, for once, wasn't crying.

"Don't you ever knock?" she said.

Harris, feeling no answer was called for, gazed around the room for a subject for conversation. He felt like it.

"I see you found your cello," he said.

Dorothy's face darkened, and her eyes filled up with their familiar burden. "Get out!" she said.

Although music might have soothed the savage

breast, any reminder of the musician served only to inflame it. And almost everything reminded her.

Harris went away and drifted into the nursery, where Morgan was cleaning up his last sister, Adelaide. She began to cry.

"Why do you always come in like a ghost?" said Morgan. "Go away!"

Harris departed and vanished from the house with the mysteriousness that characterized all his movements. He walked down to the beach, reflecting that his whole life seemed to consist of unseen comings and goings. He wondered, if he vanished altogether from the face of the earth, if anybody would notice that he'd gone.

He sat down on the stones and noted, with melancholy interest, that they were a good deal harder than he was. There was no doubt that the Irishman's hurtful accusation still rankled.

Ordinarily, insults did not affect Harris, but the Irishman had offered to supplement his with injury. He had meant it, and Harris had been impressed.

So had he only yielded to the threat of being punched into the middle of next week? Had he just been frightened? He looked around, half hoping to see the Irishman, as the middle of next week, however he reached it, offered more attractions than here and now.

It was half past six. He wondered how long he'd need to stay out before somebody came to look for him and tell him that supper was ready.

No one came. The sky grew dark and the huge sea frittered itself in a fringe of silver and sighed over the expense. The stars came out and winked at Harris, as if to mock him with their remoteness.

He frowned and tried to make out which of the tiny pricks of light was Pigott's comet. He stared from one to another, trying to detect a scrap of movement, till his eyes watered with the effort. But the stars played blindman's buff with him, so he got up and went home.

He had lost everything, even the comet. It was as if the telescope, in its death agony, had turned and struck down even its most devoted admirer. Harris had lost Bostock, too.

"Bosty!" sighed Harris, expiring in sleep. "Dear old friend!"

Chapter Eighteen

THE day that Harris had schemed for, that Bostock had yearned for, that Dorothy had sobbed for, and that Maggie Hemp had had such agonizing suspicions about dawned in heedless splendor.

It was rather like a guest who, not having been told that the party's off, arrives in foolish magnificence, at a house in tears.

First Dorothy awoke, from a dream of dancing on the top of Devil's Dyke with Philip Top-Morlion—to the unspeakable envy of Maggie Hemp—and wished herself back asleep again.

Next, Maggie Hemp awoke, from a dream of a world without slyness, in which she danced on the top of Devil's Dyke with a youth of spotless honesty—to the unspeakable envy of Dolly Harris—and *she* wished herself asleep again.

Bostock awoke from dancing on top of Devil's Dyke with Mary Harris, and *he* wished himself back asleep again. And Cassidy, in a small room at the Black Lion in Patcham, awoke from a dream of dancing all the way back to Dublin with Mary Flatley on his arm, and *he* wished himself asleep again.

Even Harris, who'd had the most horrible nightmare of being shut up inside the telescope with the Irishman, Captain Bostock, Pigott's comet, and various invisible slimy things—all of which had hostile intentions toward him—awoke and wished he hadn't. Anything was better than the emptiness of the coming day.

He tried to think, to scheme, to devise some means of renewing his hopes and saving his friendship without loss of face, but it was in vain. His thoughts rose, only to fall back exhausted, like a bird with a broken wing. He had the feeling that he was fluttering against a huge black wall, as if he had reached the end of the universe.

He went to the window and looked out, hoping that Bostock would be there. He wasn't. Harris put on his crumpled clothes, which gave him the odd appearance of having been discarded, and went downstairs.

His sister Dorothy passed him on the first landing. She was on her way to her mother's room to borrow scent and whatever else she could find that would suit her rather more than a lady of Mrs. Harris's advanced years.

She vanished quietly and Mary Harris darted across the landing on an identical errand to Dorothy's room. At such times every woman's most urgent needs turn out to be in the possession of another.

Harris went down to the kitchen where his mother

was supervising the filling of hampers and baskets for the evening's outing.

His mood darkened at the festive sight. He breakfasted frugally on a veal pie and wondered about going out. Then he remembered the Irishman, and his blood ran cold. The fellow was probably lying in wait for him with a pistol or a cudgel.

Although Harris had returned the telescope, Cassidy couldn't have known and would probably hit him without waiting for an explanation. Harris, in addition to his other misfortunes, was virtually a prisoner in his own home.

He went back upstairs, noting, without interest, that Caroline was crying. He looked out of his window. No Bostock.

He heard the front door open and bang shut. A moment later he saw Mary, in a white dress with green ribbons, scamper up the street, like a stick of celery.

He looked toward the villa on the corner. The green dress was gone. He could just make out vague movements in the window. He missed the telescope more than ever.

Mary came back, flushed and windy. She saw her brother looking down and put out her tongue. Still no sign of Bostock.

The morning continued with idle comings and goings, but Harris stayed where he was, his mood fluctuating between anger, bitterness, sadness, and despair.

Soon after midday he went down to the kitchen and removed another pie. Caroline was still crying.

At about two o'clock he saw Andrews, the fishmonger's son, call at the villa and wait at the side door till Mary Flatley appeared. She was wearing the green dress and was carrying a basket. Andrews put a small bag into it. It was his contribution to the feast. They walked off in the general direction of Devil's Dyke.

Harris tried to make a phantom of his mind and send it into Bostock's house to tap him on the shoulder and bid him come.

"Bosty! Bosty, old friend!"

No Bostock. Instead, he saw the Top-Morlion family, all in their pony cart, proceeding along the road at the top of the street.

Mrs. Top-Morlion, who was excessively tall and thin, held the reins. She sat bolt upright and, with her long neck and small round head, looked uncannily like a treble clef, driving. Monsieur Top-Morlion, who had recovered from his illness, cuddled his cello, and Philip, in addition to his fiddle, flute, and music case, was clutching a bouquet of music stands. They too were moving in the general direction of Devil's Dyke.

At half past three Maggie Hemp arrived, in a state of black and silver satin and tearful indignation. She wondered if there would be room for her in Dr. Harris's carriage?

She was not going with her ma and pa even if it meant walking all the way. Her pa was taking a whole hamper of cooked mutton chops and was going to sell them, like a common tradesman.

Maggie had never been so ashamed in all her life. It was just as if Dr. Harris were to take pills and things.

As it was, all the town seemed comet mad. Even Mr. Collier was selling marzipan comets at threepence each, and that little shop next to Saunders' was selling special smoked spectacles for viewing the comet in comfort, while the greengrocer's and the fishmonger's were all selling rides on their carts, at two shillings there and back.

It turned out that there was room in the Harrises' carriage as Mary and Caroline had quarreled and Caroline wasn't going. Maggie Hemp subsided and told Dorothy it was a pity she wasn't wearing her gray dress as the blue one she'd put on rather clashed with Maggie's hat, but there was still time to change, and didn't Dolly think she'd overdone the scent?

At five o'clock the Harris family, with the exception of Adelaide, Caroline, and Harris himself, piled into the little carriage, along with baskets, hampers, and warm blankets.

Mournfully Harris watched them. He thought of running downstairs and confessing to Mary that Bosty had not found somebody else. He felt, in some strange way, that he'd interfered with Providence, and that, if he undid what he'd done, then Providence would relent and set everything to rights.

But this was all nonsense, and Harris, the scientist, knew it. Fate, Providence, and Hostages to Fortune were all in the realm of magic. Harris was above such things, and with a shrug and a frown he conquered his impulse to confess.

The carriage departed, leaving Harris behind, with a victory as joyful as ashes. Caroline was still crying.

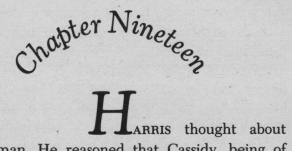

Chapter Nineteen

HARRIS thought about the Irishman. He reasoned that Cassidy, being of Celtic blood and of a violent temper, was unlikely to be possessed of much patience. Therefore, if the fellow had really been lying in wait for him, he'd have shown his hand by now.

He looked up and down the street. No hand. Cautiously he left the house and proceeded to the corner. His reasoning proved correct. Cassidy was nowhere to be seen.

Happily Harris bolted around to Bostock's and knocked loudly on the door. How much better it was, he thought, to show such generosity to Bostock by making the first move, instead of remaining at home in a somber resentment that nobody could see.

Bostock would be so overcome by the loftiness of Harris's spirit that he could hardly refuse him admission to the Crow's Nest and the use of his pa's telescope to behold the glory of Pigott's comet. Everything was for the best, after all!

The housekeeper came. Harris smiled.

"No need to ring the bell," he said. "I'll go straight up."

"Oh, no, you won't."

"Why not?"

"Because he's gone out."

"OUT?"

"Out."

"Where?"

"Up to Devil's Dyke. Didn't you know?"

Harris made a stupendous effort to control himself.

"Oh, yes—yes. Of course. I—I forgot," he said.

In no circumstances could he expose the fact that Bostock had actually done something without his, Harris's, knowledge, and that he hadn't arranged.

"I—I expect he's waiting for me," said Harris, and tottered away with a despairing jauntiness. "He'll be wondering what's happened to me. Ha—ha!"

He went back to his house. He looked into the stone coffin, not for Bostock, but in the hope of finding some scrap of graveyard philosophy to sustain him . . . such as, we are all food for worms, and what does anything matter anyway? In a hundred years who would care whether Bostock had betrayed Harris or not?

Not much comforted, he went inside the house. Morgan, who had been feeding Adelaide, shouted to him not to bang the door. But, as he'd already banged it, her remark seemed unnecessary.

Everything was unnecessary. He began to mount the stairs. Caroline was still crying. He went toward her room with the general idea of being disagreeable. He had no pity for her. She was a female and Harris loathed and despised all females. They always caused trouble and never seemed to get the blame. He opened her door.

"Go away!" sobbed Caroline.

She was sitting on her bed, holding a doll, and with her eyes as red as poppies.

"Shut up!" said Harris sternly.

Caroline's face crumpled up, as if an invisible fist were squeezing it to get more tears from her eyes. She looked very small and insignificant. Harris felt vaguely touched and inquired as to the source of her grief.

More tears and a frantic rocking of her doll, who persisted in smiling glassily. Harris told her to pull herself together.

It turned out that Caroline's grief proceeded from an undying hatred for her sister Mary. Mary, it seemed, had inexplicably wished to disassociate herself from Caroline. She had threatened to punch Caroline in the stomach and scratch her eyes out if Caroline so much as came anywhere near her once they got to Devil's Dyke.

Harris nodded; he understood both points of view. For the first time in his life he found himself sympathizing with two of his sisters at the same time. He thought.

"I'll take you," he said. "We'll walk up to the Dyke together." It had occurred to him that, by producing Caroline on top of Devil's Dyke, he would be destroying Mary's happiness, probably destroying Caroline's, and he would be discomforting Bostock by catching him out. In short, he would be killing a large number of birds with one stone. Also, he wanted very much to go to Devil's Dyke, and he was feeling so lonely that even his small sister's company was better than none.

"What are you doing with Miss Caroline?" demanded Morgan, coming out of the nursery with Adelaide under her arm.

"He's taking me up to the party on Devil's Dyke," said Caroline, proudly clutching her brother's sleeve.

"Now don't you go and lose her!" said Morgan, her wild Welsh mind muddled with ancient memories of changelings and foundlings and lostlings on the downs. "And don't bang that door!"

Devil's Dyke was five miles off and uphill every weary step of the way. Long before they were halfway there, Harris yearned to realize Morgan's worst fears and lose his bitterly complaining sister for good. She was hungry, she was thirsty, her toe hurt, and there was a tickling in one of her ears—had an animal gotten in?

Harris poked his finger in, and Caroline shrieked. They went on. Caroline hated Harris, and Harris hated Caroline; nevertheless they clung together as it was beginning to get dark.

At about seven o'clock they passed the old inn before the top of the Dyke itself. Already fires had been lighted, for the downs were chilly when the sun went down, and it was still only April.

Smoke was rising from the high place where, long ago, the Devil had stood and scooped out the deep, precipitous Dyke that was meant to let the sea come rushing in and drown all the churches of the Weald. It was as if his footprints were still hot.

There was a red glow in the air and a throng moved against it, mysteriously black. Then a wind blew. The smoke flattened and a million golden sparks danced and raced, as if Pigott's comet, to signify its arrival, had shaken out its tail.

A pleasant smell of cooked food was wafted across the downs, together with the cheerful sounds of plates, bottles, faintly jingling harness, and the pigmy out-of-doors voices of the comet watchers, as they laughed and strolled and found best places for their feasts, around the dancing green.

"Look!" cried Caroline, dragging on Harris's sleeve. "There's Dolly with Maggie Hemp!"

Harris, much relieved, hastened to dispose of Caroline. He appeared like a specter in Dorothy's path. She halted.

"That's Ma's brooch you're wearing," said Caroline observantly. "I'll tell."

"For God's sake!" said Dorothy in a rage. "Go away!"

Nobody, she thought, can expose you to the contempt and ridicule of the whole world better than your own family!

Maggie looked at the brooch. "It *is* a little old for you, dear," she said.

Dorothy wondered why she ever went out with Maggie Hemp, who always managed to say something hurtful. She longed for the dancing to begin, even though she didn't have much hope of a partner.

"Look!" she said. "There's Mr. Top-Morlion and his family! I wonder when they'll start to play."

Maggie Hemp pulled Dorothy the other way. "Look!" she said. "There's Mr. Collier selling those comet cakes! Come along and I'll buy you one, Dolly!"

Away they went.

"Look!" shouted Caroline. "There's Mary! Over there! Look! She's with—"

But Harris was no longer by her side. He had seen not Mary but the murderous Irishman! At once the prospect of personal violence had flashed upon his inner eye, and with a faint cry of alarm he had vanished from human sight.

The abandoned Caroline began to howl and scream, but it was too late. Harris, when he vanished, vanished for good.

Cassidy also had been surprised. He kept gazing about him and seeing the familiar faces of Brighton folk, ringing the firelight like demons. He felt he was drowning all over again, and yesterday was flashing before his eyes.

He and O'Rourke, having been unable to pay their bill at the Black Lion, had been obliged to work off their debt by carrying part of the landlord's family and a stock of Patcham beer and pies "up yonder hill."

Not being geographers, they'd toiled up in all inno cence from the Patcham side. Not Sir Francis Drake himself, leaving Plymouth and then coming back to it without having turned a corner, could have been more astonished than Cassidy and O'Rourke when they beheld what they thought they'd left behind.

There was Mary Flatley herself, walking arm in arm with her Englishman, who was as tall as a lamppost, only without the shine.

All Cassidy's hopes came back to him and then were dashed when he saw the size of his rival. He longed to distinguish himself, to do something valiant—to save a life, maybe . . . hers if it could happen without putting her in danger! But it was hopeless. What could he do beside Andrews, who had everything he lacked, and a rowboat besides?

"Look!" said O'Rourke. "There's that boy who'll see ye hanged, Cassidy!"

"Where?"

"Ah, he's gone now. Most likely he's gone for the magistrate. Ye'd best keep out of the way, Cassidy!"

"I'll kill him!" said Cassidy, retreating into obscurity with a tray of Patcham Ales (None Finer). "I might as well be hanged for a boy as for a brass telescope I never had!"

So Cassidy went looking for Harris, while Harris stayed where he was, trembling and perspiring under the Top-Morlions' cart.

He saw Cassidy's stoutly gaitered legs coming near. Urgently he searched for some means of defense. He found a brick wedged under one of the wheels. He pulled it free, meaning to sell his life dearly.

Cassidy, not finding Harris—and not really wanting to—put down his tray of Patcham Ales (None Finer) and rested against the cart, while nearby the Top-Morlions tuned their instruments for the beginning of the dance.

Monsieur Top-Morlion, observing out of the corner

of his eye the tray of Patcham Ales, wondered if they were an additional tribute to the musicians—a kindly refreshment, such as was always offered in France? He put down his cello. . . .

"My God!" said Mrs. Top-Morlion, poking her son in the back with the bow of her fiddle. "Look at your father! He's done it again!"

Monsieur Top-Morlion was swaying in his chair and clutching his sensitive stomach with every appearance of agony.

"He's a pig!" said Mrs. Top-Morlion furiously. "He's just drunk a whole bottle of beer after all that wine! He's nothing but a pig!"

Monsieur Top-Morlion fell off his chair and rolled on the ground, groaning piteously.

"I'd better fetch Dr. Harris," said Philip, no less furiously. "Maybe he can give him something right away."

He hurried away to where the Harris family were settled and explained the situation. Dr. Harris came at once.

"He should never have had that beer," he said after he had examined Monsieur Top-Morlion. "I warned him about straining his stomach."

"Can't you do something, Dr. Harris?" pleaded Mrs. Top-Morlion. "Just so he can play for this evening?"

The look on her face suggested that, after that, she didn't care.

Dr. Harris said there was nothing he could do, and Mrs. Top-Morlion said it was intolerable that everybody's pleasure should be ruined because of her husband's irresponsible greed.

Dr. Harris sympathized, and, wishing to be of service to his patient's family and the company in general, suggested that, if the music wasn't very difficult, his daughter Dorothy might take the cello part. She was, after all, Monsieur Top-Morlion's pupil and would most likely do him credit.

At once Philip's heart began to beat violently. He assured Dr. Harris that the cello part was simplicity itself. A child could manage it, let alone an accomplished young lady like Miss Harris.

"I'll go and find her," said Dr. Harris.

"She's over there!" said Philip rapidly.

Dr. Harris approached his daughter.

"Really, Pa!" said Dorothy, *her* heart beating violently. "The very idea! Besides, I haven't practiced for ages. I'd just be making a fool of myself!"

Maggie Hemp agreed. Dolly couldn't possibly do it!

"On the other hand," said Dorothy, dragging Maggie toward the Top-Morlions, "I don't want to be a spoilsport. And—and you can turn the pages for me, Maggie!"

She greeted Mrs. Top-Morlion politely and looked daggers at Philip. He needn't imagine she'd come to make things up.

"We really are obliged to you, Miss Harris," said Philip icily. "I think you'll find the music is quite straightforward."

She sat down, and Mrs. Top-Morlion passed her the cello. Philip leaned over to open the music.

"Miss Hemp will turn the pages for me," said Dorothy. "There's no need for you to stand so close, Mr. Top-Morlion."

She smiled triumphantly at Maggie, who smiled uncertainly back. She didn't trust Dolly an inch.

"Are you ready, Miss Harris?"

Dorothy nodded, and they began to play, almost together. A stir went through the firelit crowd, a hastening to and fro.

Then the music launched itself into "Nancy Dawson," which children know as "My Grandmother," and two by two the dancers came, shyly and awkwardly onto the green.

"Please try to keep in time!" muttered Philip, briefly lowering his flute.

"I *am* in time!"

"Then you're out of tune!"

"Please don't criticize. I'll stop if you go on like that!"

"You should practice more."

"How can I? Nobody bothers to teach me!"

"What do you mean by that? And don't keep stopping every time you talk!"

"I wasn't stopping. That was a rest. Oh, I see—it was a smudge. If you'd come to give me my lesson that night—"

"I *did* come!"

"Philip!" said Mrs. Top-Morlion. "For goodness' sake, don't keep stopping!"

"You didn't come! I waited till—"

"I did come. And you threw water over me! *And* you called me a filthy little beast!"

"I didn't! Oh, my God! Was it you?"

"Who the devil else would be playing the cello under your window?"

"Miss Harris! Philip! Please keep playing!"

"I thought it was my brother," said Dorothy savagely, and then: "Oh, Mr. Top-Morlion, what must you have thought of me?"

"A great deal, Miss Harris!"

"Will you ever forgive me?"

Would he? He thought about it. He would. Suddenly he felt that his skin was too small to hold in the bursting happiness it contained. He felt an overwhelming desire to hop and skip and fly with Miss Harris in his arms.

Impulsively he turned to Miss Hemp, who was suddenly his most talented pupil of the flute.

"Here," he said, thrusting the instrument into her hands. "Would you mind, Miss Hemp? The music's quite easy, you know!"

Then, before Maggie Hemp could say more than "VIPER!", he released Dorothy from the cello and escorted her onto the green.

"Philip! Miss Harris!" wailed Mrs. Top-Morlion, as the dancers clumped and turned and bowed to the scraping of a single violin. "Come back!"

Too late. With the lady on his left, and his right hand holding her left, Philip led Dorothy in the dance.

Drive with the left foot; step forward on the right . . . all move around one place . . .

Dorothy floated and Dorothy flew, as she danced on the top of Devil's Dyke with Philip Top-Morlion, to the unspeakable envy of Maggie Hemp!

"Serpents! Weasels! Hyenas and goats!" sobbed Maggie Hemp as her worst suspicions came true. "I *hate* the world!"

She flung down the flute and went to sit on the back of the pony cart, to cry and cry and cry.

Unfortunately it was the very cart under which Harris was concealed, and from which he had removed the securing brick. Looking up, he was alarmed to see the cart begin to move under the tempestuous weight of Miss Hemp.

Fearing exposure, Harris began to crawl away, taking good care to choose the opposite direction from where he could still see Cassidy's feet.

In consequence of this, he was forced to brush lightly against the pony's legs. At once the ignorant beast snorted, tossed its head, and jerked its tethering post out of the ground.

Maggie Hemp screamed, and the pony, frightened out of its wits, set off briskly in the direction of the wild, plunging Dyke itself.

Cassidy, picking himself up from where he'd fallen when the cart had left him, saw at once an opportunity of distinguishing himself and shining in Mary Flatley's eyes.

"I'll save ye! I'll save ye!" he roared and stared wildly around for Mary Flatley, just to make sure she could see him.

But for God's sake, she was nowhere to be found, and there was the poor girl screaming her head off and being rattled along to her terrible death, maybe hundreds of feet down below!

"I'll save ye! I'll save ye!" yelled Cassidy frantically, and shut his eyes in terror and waited for the faraway crash!

It wasn't that he was a coward; it was just that he

was so frightened of going over the edge with the cart that he couldn't move a step.

He heard shouts, he heard cries, but, Heaven be praised, he heard no crash. He opened his eyes and saw that the cart had been stopped and the poor, weeping girl was standing upright on the ground. Who had saved her? ANDREWS!

The dirty scoundrel had poked his nose in again! He was a professional rescuer, and that's all there was to it! Poor Cassidy never stood a chance. A fellow like that would have beaten St. George himself to the dragon . . . the great big hulking lump of wood! Cassidy sat down and cried.

"Will ye not come and dance with me, Michael Cassidy?" said Mary Flatley's voice, while Mary Flatley's hand came down and stroked his hair.

He looked up, and she looked down, and there was a look in her eyes that would have raised Dublin Castle up if ever it had tumbled down.

"But—but yer friend over there?"

"He's no friend of mine, Michael Cassidy," said Mary Flatley, offering him her hand. "D'ye think I've got the time of day for a fellow that's always goin' after rescuin' and leavin' me standin' on me own?"

Cassidy stood up.

"And d'ye think, Michael Cassidy, that I've not got eyes in me head to see that ye love me truly? For wasn't it yerself that risked yer life to save me from drownin' when ye couldn't swim a stroke? So I'll never forget that it was yerself that didn't risk yer neck for *another* girl, and not him!"

They walked onto the green to join the waiting

dancers, and the lonely lady fiddler struck up again.

Hop on the left foot, step with the right; ladies turn under the gentlemen's arms. All move around one place . . .

"I don't know how to thank you," said Maggie Hemp, drying her eyes and cautiously examining her savior from beneath lowered lids. "Really I don't."

Andrews didn't know either, although he appeared to be giving the matter some thought. He felt vaguely distressed to see that he'd lost Mary Flatley and, with her, his contribution to the feast. He looked wistfully toward her as she and Cassidy danced together, like two green leaves.

"Would you—would you like to dance with me?" asked Maggie Hemp, feeling that such a sacrifice was the least she could make.

"I'm not much of a dancer, miss."

"I don't believe you!" said Maggie Hemp, taking hold of Andrews' huge hand. "I really don't!"

Onto the green they went and joined in the growing dance. Andrews tripped and stumbled and trod on Maggie's foot. Just as he'd said, he wasn't much of a dancer, but at least he'd told the truth and not been sly. *That* was something. And compared with that weedy Top-Morlion, he was a real Apollo, even though he smelled of fish. She hoped Dolly Harris could see her and go green with envy over her catch!

For a little while Harris, his danger past and his person secure, watched the revolving dancers on the green.

Hop on the right foot, step with the left . . . partners

give right hands and make a turn . . . all move around one place . . .

He turned away. Not for him the happiness of finding a partner, only the sadness of losing a friend. He looked up, hoping to catch a glimpse of the comet, which surely was as solitary as himself. But the air was too full of smoke and flying sparks.

The dance went on. Flushed faces bobbed; eyes winked like stars.

Gentlemen bow . . . and rise up on their toes . . .

Dark figures against the fire, weaving in and out . . . little shrieks as bright embers touched the hems of swinging skirts and then went out. All move around one place . . .

All but one. At the end of the line a single figure hopped and capered as if unaware that his partner had long since fled his company.

"Bosty!" shrieked Harris.

"Harris!" shouted Bostock.

Shining with delight and relief, he left the dance and rushed upon his friend. They shook hands.

"Harris!" said Bostock. "You're a genius!"

Harris blinked away a tear.

"You did it, Harris! Just as you always said. Mary danced with me . . . and I danced with Mary! Oh, Harris, Harris!"

Then, as Harris listened, Bostock told him that not only was he the most brilliant but also the most magnanimous person that he, Bostock, knew. He was ashamed, he said, to think how wonderful and forgiving Harris had been. Even though he'd asked for the telescope back, Harris had still kept his word and given him Mary.

She'd come around to his house that morning and asked him to be her companion on Devil's Dyke. Bostock had been absolutely overwhelmed by Harris's generosity. But how had he done it? How had he accomplished such a miracle?

Harris smiled and frowned and thought. How had he done it? For the moment he was not quite sure.

In point of fact, he had done it by accident. But that didn't detract from his achievement. Most great discoveries are made by accident. After all, Archimedes had meant to wash, not to soak the bathroom.

Harris had wrought his masterpiece when he'd told Mary, in a fit of anger, that Bostock had found another girl. That was all. Mary, when she'd gotten over her incredulity, wondered who it was that Bostock had found. Who would go out with that idiot? Then she fell to wondering if, perhaps, there was more to Bostock than she'd supposed. Then she'd decided she'd better try Bostock for herself in case she'd been missing something. Also she'd be hitting another girl in the eye, which was a satisfaction in itself.

So she'd secured Bostock and threatened Caroline, as she wasn't going to have that little cow laughing her head off while she danced with her brother's awful friend.

Now she'd gone, having discovered that the only aspect of Bostock to which there was more than she'd supposed had been his feet. But she *had* danced with him.

"Oh, Harris!" said Bostock, quite overcome by the memory. "How *did* you do it?"

"It was really quite simple, Bosty," said Harris, emerging from his ponderings like a sagacious retriever, with the answer in his mouth. "It was only a question of knowledge properly applied."

Quietly he explained to Bostock about the learned article and how the whole ingenious ritual of Courtship had been followed and at last fulfilled. First there'd been the display of bright plumage and the discharge of scent, then the performing of music and the presentation of prey, and finally, right on top of Devil's Dyke, had come the execution of the dance. That had done it.

It was just, said Harris shrewdly, that you had to go through the lot. There were no shortcuts. Omit one and the rest would never have followed. It was rather like a figure in a quadrille.

"To prove it," said Harris, "we could do it again if you like."

Bostock shook his head. He'd had his moment and he'd treasure it all his life. Perhaps in the future—a long way off—he'd think differently. But not now. To be honest, he was rather glad it was all over and he and Harris were friends.

They began to walk away from Devil's Dyke, leaving the dance behind. Once more a great warmth of affection glowed between them, and a great depth of friendship, no matter how ruffled the surface had lately been.

At last they came to Bostock's house, and Bostock asked Harris if he'd like to come in and watch Pigott's comet through his pa's telescope, up in the Crow's Nest.

Harris said he would, and together they climbed to the top of the house. There, while Harris scoured the heavens with an eager eye, Bostock thought of Mary and the cost of her in terms of his pa's property, ruined or lost. But he wasn't worried any more. Christmas was a long way off, and Harris would be sure to think of something. Harris was a genius, after all.